# A Mad World in a Madhouse

# A Mad World in a Madhouse

## Tall Pike

Tall Pike
2018

First Printing: 2018

ISBN 978-1-9993980-1-9

All business inquiries can be sent to: tallpike@look.ca

To whom would I like to dedicate this book?
Why… to you, dear reader.
Yes, *you*!

# Chapter 1

JOHNNY TRIED HIS HARDEST not to laugh or even smirk as Dr. Saunders paced up and down before the row of patients. Standing quietly—and most of them motionlessly—they waited for the hospital's head shrink to break the awkward silence. The degree of patience they had was unnatural.

The wide white corridor in the hospital's psychiatric building seemed like such an inane place to have people standing at attention, or so Johnny thought.

Were they supposed to be in the army or something?

No matter how many times he and the other patients did this, the seriousness of the silence—which was just begging to be challenged—never ceased to give Johnny the urge to giggle.

As if he were reading Johnny's thoughts, Dr. Saunders stopped abruptly in front of him, turned, and stared into his eyes. The doctor maintained his usual courteous pretence, but it only thinly veiled his icy sternness, which strongly hinted at an underlying mean-spiritedness.

"So tell us," began Dr. Saunders slowly, using his most condescending tone. He paused before actually asking the question, so he could assume that ridiculously pompous pose of his; the one that involved folding his arms so he would appear intellectual… in a disdainful and superior sort of way.

"Tell us, Johnny: If you could become any animal at all, which animal would that be?"

He'd already asked the rest of the assembly that question, having picked the members of the queue at random. So, obviously it was Johnny's turn, even though Dr. Saunders had decided to create a needless delay with all his pacing, pausing, and giving ambivalent looks to patients whom he'd already asked. If Dr. Saunders was doing it to create an air of uncertainty about what was going to happen next, or to instil anxiety and awkwardness in the group, then his method was pathetic... especially since he made such a predictable routine of acting like a stuffy, self-important twit.

If anything, his having the patients file at attention during these meetings was the disturbing part: Was this guy really trying to make like he was a military officer? That was a bit scary, though not in the way the good doctor had probably intended.

While Johnny wasn't sure how he himself would know, he was still pretty darn suspicious that drill sergeants generally didn't come off as complete weirdoes in the way Dr. Saunders usually did.

Johnny smiled at Dr. Saunders, trying to hold back from blurting out the first thing that came to mind; the sort of thing that would have possibly caused a fuss. While he felt unusually glad to be here and excited about answering the stupid question (for a reason he couldn't explain), there were a few other things Johnny wanted to express, which were definitely better left unsaid. For now, he'd just have to hold on to his self-induced eagerness to participate.

Unfortunately, he'd unwittingly gone a step further than making himself look forward to Dr. Saunders's experimental little group... thing (whatever it was). Johnny had managed to pull off such a radical adjustment to his attitude that this session was now bringing him the kind of excitement he had to contain.

"A griffin!" he exclaimed, beaming cheerily. He had to admit, he was rather proud of being able to give such a creative answer. "Ask me why! Ask me why!"

Looking at him with a raised eyebrow, Dr. Saunders said nothing.

After five seconds, Johnny decided to skip waiting for a verbal response:

"See, a griffin's this eagle-lion thingy who must be as confused about its identity as I am about mine!" he proclaimed. "I mean, am I bird or a mammal? If I were female, would I lay eggs or give birth to live young?"

Finding Dr. Saunders's lack of amusement funnier than his own witticism, Johnny let out an involuntary titter. Though he was feeling far from nervous or awkward, he could hear what sounded like self-consciousness in his manic giggle.

His odd little laugh had also partially come from having mentioned and thus having thought about his state of confusion; though, he wasn't sure why he should find it funny all of a sudden.

Still, that must have been it.

Confused he certainly was; he would support that before truly accepting the idea that he'd been as mad as a hatter when he'd first come here.

Dr. Saunders didn't respond verbally; he just gave Johnny a blank look that only thinly dampened the underlying glare. It was the kind of expression that usually terrified Johnny, but not today. (Granted, he'd done more than just brainwashed himself into accepting whatever stupidity or menace the day would bring; he'd convinced himself to dive into it gleefully.)

Then, while the row of patients continued to wait quietly for their marching orders, Dr. Saunders began pacing again. If past patterns were any indication, Dr. Saunders would waste time for a good ten minutes or so, as if to breed tension and drive everyone nuts (or nuttier than they'd already been branded to be).

Johnny just tuned it out, taking the opportunity for a bout of introspection, which the topic of his confusion had just inspired:

He didn't know exactly when his issues had started. Several problems had surfaced gradually, building up over a period of years before eventually congealing into a big and messy one. While his memory still had the capacity to access the final months leading to his stay here, he usually forbid it from doing such a horrible thing. (He sometimes wondered if this part-time, self-imposed memory loss could become permanent, if he forced it to continue for too long.)

After realizing that these people were not going to help him with his issues, there'd just been no point to examining the past... beyond his periodic need to take a quick glimpse in order to compare the details of what he knew with what the staff had insisted to be true.

That was where that whole confusing identity issue came in; people here were always telling him details about his past that he knew weren't true. (He hardly needed to think consciously about the details he wanted to banish from his memory to know a fallacy when he heard one.) Worse than that, they couldn't keep their account of his history straight; they were constantly changing their story of who he was and why he was really here.

If they weren't making inconsistent stuff up, then he really was bananas. The main reason for his stay at the hospital would then be obvious, even if beyond the grasp of his perception.

While the doctors and nurses frowned upon the use of words like "madness" or "madman"—even when Johnny flippantly applied them to himself—the way they treated him rendered any admonishment of his wording pretty darn hypocritical. If they were going to talk down to him as though he were a madman, then they might as well have called him one outright...

They had quite a disdainful and sometimes-hostile air whenever he insisted that he could recall the process of being voluntarily registered as a patient here, which was in direct conflict with their narrative. According to them, he'd been brought here involuntarily and committed because he'd done things he couldn't remember. Their assertions entailed an issue far worse than just a failing memory; Johnny had a completely different account of events, which he'd grown too tired of examining to think about now.

If they were right or their attitude was justified, then they might as well have called him a lunatic and a weirdo; it would have been more honest than their patronizing and scornful attempts to tell him that he didn't know what he was talking about. (As much as he didn't like thinking about his experiences with people on the outside, he remembered that they'd been a lot like the staff in that way.)

Maybe that was another, possibly unconscious reason why Johnny had willingly—and eagerly—banished his past from his mind: Dwelling on it too much, alongside all the garbage that people like Dr. Saunders had so obstinately fed him, would only add to his confusion.

Did Dr. Saunders want Johnny to erase his sense of identity and accept whatever ridiculous substitute the doctor shoved down his throat? While Johnny wasn't ready to commit to any theory, he couldn't rule out the idea that he was the subject of some kind of wicked experiment, which was a thought he was still sane enough to keep to himself.

Deciding to do without the emotional baggage (which the past sustained), he was just "Johnny" now; he'd shut out his other names, middle and last. (He really hated his full name these days, and did whatever he could to avoid using it.)

No one here used his last name, and he had no visitors of any kind, friends or family. Without even having to think about his big circle of acquaintances—whom he didn't want to think about—he wasn't shocked that none of them had bothered to check up on him thus far. He was a bit surprised that no one among his relatives had bothered to show up, though; still, he couldn't remember ever feeling sad or disappointed about it.

In the end, the absence of people from his past made forgetting them simple. If they were going to abandon him like that, perhaps doing so was for the best. It was just another component of his past erased, which added room in his mind for his immediate circle of acquaintances (whatever that was worth).

Maybe it was unkind for him to get so frustrated, but he really had to hold back from angrily dismissing the other patients as lost causes, even if they were more demented than he allegedly was. All of them were unreceptive, bordering on vegetative, and there was no talking to them about anything.

The weird part was, new arrivals to this place—no matter how manically lively or brimming with upset they were initially—would always end up acting like mute drones within a week or two.

Sometimes, he'd start to feel antagonized by the behaviour of his fellow patients, before reminding himself that these people were harmless, and that his impulse to feel hostility towards them was unreasonable and maybe a little mean-spirited. Really, his part-time temptation to write them off as lunatics and weirdoes came out of frustration, as opposed to an inclination to look down on them for having whatever issues they did. His failed attempts to bond with people here had only accentuated how alone he was in this whole thing, as selfish as it might have been for him to think in those terms. It was easy to perceive their acting like he didn't exist as snobbery or disdain, and their quiet passivity as indifference to everything. It didn't do much to alleviate his nerves when everyone who wasn't a staff member behaved exactly the same way, and always obeyed the wishes of Dr. Saunders with robotic precision.

Johnny also hated (and avoided) thinking about the schools he'd gone to, and whatever he'd gone through while attending them. The same feeling applied to any of the jobs he'd had; skilled, semiskilled, or unskilled. So long as he was Johnny from the Asylum, none of that stuff mattered anyway; he might as well have had no schooling or jobs.

Everyone who'd been dropped off here had been abandoned, and Johnny seemed to be the only one who'd noticed.

Stripped down to the bare bones of your existence in here, only your character defined you. It didn't matter how prestigious your career was (or how prestigious you thought it was), or whatever else you thought you'd had on the outside. After being whittled down to their core essence, lawyers, dishwashers, kings, and paupers ceased to have distinction from one another.

No one was going to squabble over whose life was the most impressive, or whose profession was the most skilled or important (which was actually an upside to being here, since braggarts were annoying). There was no bickering about status of any kind, since none of the patients had any connection to anyone or anything outside the hospital, including visitors (which was actually a little weird). In a place cut off from the world—a place where such matters of identity were no longer acknowledged—you had nothing left but your body, soul, and what was left of your mind to rely on. When those things went, you were in real trouble; what you did to preserve them was the only thing that mattered now, the only personal distinction you could develop and maintain.

For that reason, disowning things that were only relevant in another life had seemed rational to Johnny. Heck, it had already been the desirable thing to do.

Other personal details he'd successfully shunned from his memory included his age and his birthday. Having dispensed with so much else, why fret over details that just weren't worth worrying about anymore? He'd already lost track of how long he'd been here, so forgetting those things were easy, too.

Eventually, he'd started slipping into sporadic periods of genuine forgetfulness, probably from keeping the details of his life out of his head for so long. He'd panicked a little at first, but over time he'd actually come to enjoy moments when he really felt ageless and without a past; it was, after all, the only real alternative to having a past he wanted to forget.

(Johnny refused to accept any of the counterfeit histories Dr. Saunders kept trying to push on him.)

Occasionally, he wondered if he would eventually forget facts about himself, completely and permanently. Keeping them out of his mind for so long, a few of them might have been beyond his capacity to remember already, though he didn't dig very deep into his memory to find out for sure. Except for Dr. Saunders's blatant lies about his history, nobody went out of their way to remind Johnny of anything about himself, which he'd instantly recognize as true. Everyone, including Dr. Saunders, only referred to him as "Johnny," and no one, especially Dr. Saunders, ever wished him a happy birthday.

(Though he didn't really worry about it, Johnny still wondered what information these people had bothered to include in their patient records, if they even kept them.)

At least a couple of times, he'd played a little game with himself in his mode of self-inflicted pseudo-amnesia, partially to distract himself from his other stresses and partially to see how he perceived the stranger he'd become in his own eyes:

Looking in a mirror, he'd observe a wild-eyed, scrawny guy in his mid-twenties staring back at him. Even though he looked unhealthy, with dark rings under his big bright green eyes, he figured he was handsome enough... or so he liked to think. He supposed he could have been a well-preserved specimen of a man in his late twenties, or perhaps even older. There was also the remote possibility that he was actually a sad example of a horribly-aged teenager (though enough of his mostly-suppressed memories still lingered in his awareness to insist otherwise).

His longish hair was always messy, bringing to mind a hyperactive sort who was always on the go with no particular destination in mind.

Once, someone in here had told Johnny that he looked like an unhealthier, slightly younger, and unkempt version of Dr. Saunders; a virtual twin who didn't wear the doctor's thick glasses. Angry beyond words at such an offensive remark, Johnny had forced himself to forget who'd actually made it.

Johnny quickly ousted that particular thought from his mind.

The doctors and nurses didn't seem to have a problem with Johnny's wired appearance (which, Johnny insisted, had no resemblance to Dr. Saunders). To the contrary, some of the staff seemed to find his appearance and some of his outbursts amusing, though Dr. Saunders was never one of them. Like Dr. Saunders, albeit in a different way, a few of his underlings seemed to encourage whatever mental maladies he had, hoping to get a cheap laugh out of his extroverted modes.

Dr. Saunders and the rest of his subordinates, meanwhile, seemed to look at Johnny as though he were the subject of some sadistic experiment. Acting outwardly displeased, they'd do and say things that he often interpreted as attempts to drive him even crazier than he already was (supposedly).

Usually, his behaviour didn't really need much encouraging. In spite of himself, he'd landed in trouble on a regular basis, even when he'd refrained from letting loose with his impulsive and (he had to admit) obnoxious behaviour; that typically came when he asked too many questions about his meds or what his treatment was supposed to achieve.

Disciplinary action was also puzzlingly inconsistent: If he got on a crusty nurse's nerves with his irritating remarks or fits of giggles, he'd sometimes get locked in his quarters for the rest of the day without any prior warning. If he innocuously questioned or tactfully criticized Dr. Saunders's ideas, he'd usually receive the worst of the punishments this place had to offer, which made Johnny uncomfortable to think about.

The staff's response to disobedience was a crapshoot, which made his defiance a gamble, as well as something he'd felt compelled to experiment with. Sometimes, he'd get locked up in his room—or worse—as a punishment for not taking his medication. (Although he'd honestly forgotten about the stuff from time to time, there were moments when he'd refused to consume the latest pill or capsule the doctor had given him, not feeling comfortable with it. In either case, some form of "discipline" would still come Johnny's way.) Johnny would also get similar punishments for arguing with Dr. Saunders about the details of Johnny's history, which was both senseless and frightening. Meanwhile, he'd just get a lengthy scolding for what was deliberately unruly behaviour, like this one time he'd thrown a crumpled paper ball at the back of a nurse's head, wanting to see what would happen.

Even after he'd tried again, replacing the paper ball with a rubber one, the reproach was still pretty mild. The angry reprimands were no harsher than what a grade school teacher would give a disruptive student; the kind of class clown he sometimes wished he'd had the wit to pull off when he was a kid. While he'd dumped a lot of his memories of actually being in a grade school classroom, he could still bring the typical imagery to mind with a little help from his imagination.

Once upon a time, early in his life as a patient, Johnny would have been the first to say that a guy really needed his imagination in here, so he could at least keep himself entertained. His attraction to using his imagination had ended the moment it had taken to using him, as if to amuse itself at his expense. He couldn't be sure that his senses really were wonky when he'd see, hear, smell, and even touch things that shouldn't have been there, but the only other possibility he could think of entailed his living in an otherworldly place, which had no stable laws of physics. He wasn't sure if he could handle the idea that reality was bending and shifting in ways that defied reason, as if to aid Dr. Saunders on his quest to keep Johnny mad.

Johnny's first episode of what could have been a state of psychosis came after a particularly heated argument with Dr. Saunders, during one of their private one-on-one meetings. His wicked imagination had augmented Dr. Saunders's disciplinary measures, turning an already unreasonable and unorthodox punishment into something gruelling for him to endure, making it by far the worst of the punitive measures Dr. Saunders had meted out so far.

To think, all Johnny had done, essentially, was point out the fact that Dr. Saunders had kept changing Johnny's prescription and his appraisal of Johnny's mental health... while denying that he'd ever made any such revisions. (Now Dr. Saunders had Johnny on these little orange pills, which he had to take under threat... so maybe it was just as well he didn't know what this latest medication was for.)

Up until the moment he'd introduced Johnny to the particularly cruel penalty, Dr. Saunders hadn't even given him a clear ultimatum or warning; just a few condescending and dismissive statements before sending him straight to the Quiet Room, or, as Johnny liked to call it, the Hole.

To this day, Johnny couldn't say just where or what the Hole was, since he'd always get a rather painful injection to put him under while he was being carted off there. Then he'd wake up alone in a place that would actually make him miss even the company of Dr. Saunders. Always afforded plenty of time to try to find his way out of the Hole, Johnny had never managed to succeed. He'd only be removed from it after he'd passed out from exhaustion; regaining consciousness, he'd find himself back in his quarters, lying atop his bed.

He imagined that the so-called Quiet Room (which was a lot more than just a single room) was probably located somewhere on the hospital grounds, which included a few separate (and usually old) buildings in addition to the sanatorium.

All he knew about the Hole—other than the fact that he feared returning to it whenever the subject came up—was that it was a sinister place where Johnny's imaginings became so vivid that they would seem to come to life... or so he'd try to convince himself whenever he was actually there. When he was away from the Hole, Johnny wasn't sure how many of his experiences there had been imaginary. Sure, his crazy mind might have spiced up the threatening atmosphere, exaggerating what he'd thought he'd seen and heard, but he couldn't quite dismiss the reality of at least a few of those things. He'd spent more time than he cared to calculate trying to figure out which of the Hole's apparent torments had been real, and which had been completely imaginary.

Many of the happenings could have been half-imaginary; that was to say, his unreliable senses could have twisted his perception of occurrences, which might have had an otherwise obvious natural explanation. When you had an illness that distorted your interpretation of the world around you, anything you were exposed to could seem to take on terrifying, supernatural qualities.

It wouldn't have surprised Johnny to think that Dr. Saunders's minions were manipulating events in the Hole, taking advantage of Johnny's fragile state of mind. They could play tricks on him from behind a curtain, so to speak, if Johnny wasn't fit to detect the source of the chicanery.

Still, whenever he'd tried clinging to that theory while in the Hole, he'd have his doubts about it once things got too intense, which they always did. Of course, Johnny's angry shouts for Dr. Saunders to knock off his little magic show had gone unanswered, making for a futile gesture of defiance.

Johnny could feel himself beginning to tremble at the memory of those experiences, which shook him out of his reverie. Dr. Saunders was still pacing in front of the assembly, posturing his authority and wasting everyone's time, so, while avoiding memories of the Hole itself, Johnny allowed himself to slip back into his mental wanderings...

As if the Hole wasn't bad enough, Johnny was absolutely certain that he hadn't started hallucinating until after he'd visited that place a few times, contrary to what he'd been told. As far as he could tell, the strange things he'd experienced inside the Hole had eventually followed him out of it. Sure, the multi-sensory illusions (if that's what they were) were never constant or as threatening as they were whenever he was in the Hole, but they'd definitely been out of the ordinary for Johnny... even if Dr. Saunders had continually insisted otherwise.

Even when he was willing to consider Dr. Saunders's lofty talk about Johnny's tendency to have "psychotic episodes," he'd still wonder if something had been done to him from too many stays in the doctor's Not-So-Quiet Room. Perhaps something there had permanently damaged his mind.

(He wondered if he really was crazy for also considering the remote possibility that the Hole was haunted and its evil spirits had decided to pursue him wherever he would go, clinging to his personal space like a sticky turd.)

Naturally, Johnny had refrained from being disruptive in any way for quite a while after his first stay in the Hole. Still, he'd eventually returned to his silly antics, gradually losing care and subtlety about his behaviour as time went on. Shielding his memory from the traumatic experience, he'd forget what he'd been so afraid of. Sometimes he'd catch himself about to do something stupid and realize that distancing himself from any brutal consequences just put him in danger of facing them again.

Johnny thought about that a moment: Sure, it would have been pretty low of him if he were worried about consequences instead of any wrongdoing that brought them. The thing was, Johnny honestly couldn't think of anything he'd done that could be classically defined as "wrongdoing." After thinking long and hard about the subject, he remained almost certain that he hadn't done anything that warranted the kind of punishment Dr. Saunders seemed to enjoy giving him, even if he enjoyed it quietly.

The crazy thing was, those silly antics were never what got him sent to the Hole...

Ever since Johnny's first (but not last) session of enduring the Hole, Dr. Saunders would respond to even the most politely-asked (but "wrong") questions with overt threats instead of proper answers. At least, that's what happened on good days, when Dr. Saunders wouldn't just have him put back there without any kind of warning. Sometimes, Dr. Saunders would just accuse Johnny of refusing to cooperate without defining whatever uncooperative thing he had supposedly done.

If Johnny ever challenged the assertion that he needed to be taught a lesson—or used the wrong tone when asking why he'd just been punished—well then he'd get a second trip to the Hole, sometimes not an hour from the end of his first one.

Reflecting on his predicament—his having to stay in the sanatorium at all—was now souring his mood. In moments like this, when his resentment and despair began to creep up to the surface of his consciousness, his giddiness would fade and his then-unclouded mind would think the most austere and overwhelming things.

Whenever he entered even a partial state of serious-mindedness, he would usually feel inspired to plan his escape from this place.

Sometimes, he would practice sneaking away from the psychiatric hospital, testing his stealth with little experiments of sneaking throughout the sanatorium. Often, he would manage to venture outside and into the other hospital buildings with ease. Although he would sometimes creep out of his quarters after lights-out, he tended to test his ability to slip away from a crowd unnoticed.

Typically, Johnny would try breaking away from the assembly of patients, who were taking part in a group activity alongside him. Usually there were between fifteen and twenty patients to a group, though he never bothered to count them. The exact number of people fluctuated from session to session. Every session brought together a new combination of people, which made him wonder if they'd been randomly selected from the patient roster.

Thus far, every group had included those whom he'd seen recently and those whom he hadn't seen for ages (in a group session or otherwise). Every so often, he'd also see one or two faces he'd never seen before, whether or not they'd actually belonged to new patients. Typically, new patients were characterized by their liveliness, which they'd always exhibited when first arriving.

Meanwhile, a couple of faces would disappear over time, though nobody had ever said anything about anyone leaving the sanatorium for good. Johnny himself had never really noticed the absence of any particular patient until he'd thought about it much later.

The inconsistent mix and number of people from group to group made it easy for a person to lose track of who was in it on any particular day. Dr. Saunders always knew who was supposed to attend his meetings, but his underlings didn't seem to pay attention to such things.

A nurse and a detachment of security guys would usually herd the patients outside for a break, or, after a meeting with Dr. Saunders, absently take them for a long walk across the hospital grounds. Not once did the staff make a show of taking a headcount before bringing the group back inside the psychiatric building. At times like those, Johnny's temptation to practice the art of escape was at its peak.

He was always a little surprised that the staff never seemed to notice (or care) whenever he would dart away from the procession. On at least a couple of those occasions, he should have been caught falling out of line, and yet no one had said or done a thing. Instead, the staff—and those under their care—had casually continued on their not-so-merry way.

It had occurred to him that they'd been indulging him, thinking he was playing some little game and leaving him to it. Therefore, he'd eventually decided to play along with their playing along with him...

Mentally immersing himself in the role, he would sometimes embrace the childish fantasy of becoming a ninja or thief in the night (while in broad daylight). Knowing how ridiculous he looked, he would make theatrical movements while flitting from one place of partial-concealment to the next, mimicking sweeping and swishing sound effects with his mouth, exaggerating his lip movements. He would take cover against walls in corridors or behind furniture while indoors, and use things like trees, bushes, or even garbage cans to hide behind while outside. Johnny would always make a point of darting his eyes back and forth before moving to his next spot. Upon reaching a new position, he would then assume a goofy martial arts stance, which had been a caricature of a caricature from a cartoon or movie.

Initially, he'd decided that he'd take advantage of his nutter status and make a guise out of it. His acting like a reality-detached fool killed any need to explain anything to anyone if he got caught wandering around. However, there were two aspects of his clownish persona: One side of him consciously used pretences of buffoonery to either fool the staff or toy with them, when he was angry and fed up with their crap. The other side of him, which emerged from his psyche uncontrollably and sporadically, was every bit the fool he would otherwise pretend to be.

Unfortunately, that meant his goofball mode could sometimes cease to be a disguise shortly after he'd adopted it. After enjoying a little adventure, whether it was sneaking away from his captors or being disruptive, he could quickly revert to his regressive ditzy mode without consciously realizing it. In fact, the transition was so erratic that sometimes he didn't have to start off pretending to be a silly or even a hyperactive twit for the persona to take its hold on him.

While trying to see how far away from the psychiatric building he could get, he would lose himself in the fun-loving persona, get distracted, and end up wandering around the compound with the unfocused desire to explore.

True, he had to admit that a part of him craved the kind of excitement he would never get in here if he hadn't gotten a little juvenile from time to time; the same could be said for his disruptive outbursts and the like. Even when he did fearfully think about what they could do to him, he couldn't deny it: Something about seeing the staff annoyed really brought a smile to his face. Those who found his obnoxious behaviour amusing weren't on the receiving end of it, unlike the few who'd tried their best to withhold any sign of feeling irritated. To everyone else's laughter, targets of his mischief would always end up snapping at him after a long period of visibly straining to ignore him.

Still, Johnny failed to understand this uncontrollable impulse of his, which essentially amounted to defying his own escape plans. His tendency to embrace his love of fooling around really begged one question: Did he really want to get out of here or didn't he?

While he was sure his fits of hyper-flightiness had only started after he'd been imprisoned in the psychiatric hospital, they really made him wonder if he could ever function in normal society. Even if his unbalanced condition wasn't rooted in the underlying reason he'd first been committed, his capricious state (or states) of mind gave Dr. Saunders a legitimate and arguably objective reason to keep Johnny here, or at least away from the public unmonitored.

That thought was as horrible as it was plausible, since Dr. Saunders had already abused his position by spewing lie after lie—and flimsy diagnosis after flimsy diagnosis—at Johnny. Simply because he was Dr. Saunders, he had control of the official narrative, which was a fact he hadn't hesitated to take advantage of already. His routinely rewriting Johnny's psychological profile—in order to suit some abusive agenda— was evidence enough of this.

Even without any credence to fuel his reasoning, Dr. Saunders's attitude and actions were bad enough. Johnny really had to remember that the doctor's behaviour would likely worsen the moment it was given one iota of justification.

So far, Johnny had managed to ditch all the goofy theatrics whenever he'd tried sneaking outside the building at night, at times when the lights were out and all the other patients were abed. The first time he'd tried to escape under those circumstances, he'd been boxed in with about twenty others. For that entire week, they'd been forced to share a disused ward in the sanatorium, because some of the patients' quarters had needed maintenance.

Before that week, the ward hadn't been used in decades. Supposedly, it had fallen into disuse when the psychiatric building had ceased to be a part of the regular hospital. The place had proven to be gloomy well before lights-out, with its cracked and water-damaged walls and concrete floor. To either side of the room, a row of ten beds lined the long walls in the typical layout of a ward; a wide empty floor between the rows made an aisle between the small doorway on one end of the room and a rusty old radiator and a barred window decorating the other.

On that pivotal night, he'd been unable to take the atmosphere or lack of privacy anymore, and his foul mood had finally inspired him to try leaving undetected. Oh sure, dark curtains had been drawn around each of the small beds, concealing their occupants from one another, but still… He'd hated being kept awake from the cold, as well as the weird grumbles that weren't coming from any of the other beds. He'd also grown fed up with nervously anticipating someone (a person, if he was lucky) violently poking his head through the bed curtains at any given moment.

After summoning the courage to peer between the curtains bordering his bed, he'd noticed that the guard sitting by the exit looked asleep. While hoping the closed curtains of the other beds were keeping Johnny as concealed from the others as they were from him, he'd instinctively found himself creeping towards the door and past the guard. All he'd had to do was keep quiet, and evade the eyes of any staff patrolling the halls…

No one had been standing right outside the ward, or anywhere in the halls; while Johnny had thought it was a little strange, he'd still welcomed the absence of people.

After completing the successful excursion without getting caught, he'd braved taking quite a few unsupervised trips at night, even after he'd gotten his quarters back. Every time, he'd managed to sneak outside and return to his bed undetected. He'd also done so without slipping into flake-mode; maybe the sobering crankiness he'd felt during his first time escaping after lights-out had stayed with him.

Memories of the outings came to mind as an overlapping collective. He usually didn't bother to sort them into specific times unless he really had to.

The property within the hospital compound was always a pleasant place for a stroll at night. The grounds were made up of a web of winding walkways, narrow roads, flowerbeds, and paved lots that divided a giant lawn; or, inversely, the grounds consisted of many lawns that divided everything else into a network of paths and whatnot. There were benches, picnic tables, and garbage cans near the entrances to some of the surrounding buildings; there were also a few in the centre of the area, which had been decorated with hedges, a couple of trees, patches of colourful flowers, and a big fountain.

Even when reality hadn't been working quite right in Johnny's perception, the grounds had still gone easy on his senses. One night, he could've sworn he'd seen a pond where the fountain usually was. A furry, pink moose had been quietly sipping its waters before it had noticed Johnny staring at it. After raising its head and giving him a dirty glare, the beast with the cotton candy hide had stood up on its hind legs and walked away indignantly.

Johnny had slowly made his way towards the pond to take a close look at it; he'd dipped his hand in the water, which had definitely been cold and wet, and touched the surrounding rocks and weeds. The pond had proven to be as real to his senses as anything could ever be, and yet the fountain had reappeared the next day, standing where it always had.

There'd been a few incidents like that, proving that Johnny was still susceptible to what typically happened in the psych building, especially in the Hole. A few times he'd witnessed freaky things that defied the reality he'd thought he lived in: Other strange animals he couldn't even begin to describe sitting by the fountain or on the benches, or large animate plants that chatted to one another in foreign languages. One time, he'd watched the night sky become empty of stars, which had begun falling in silent showers of comets.

Other times, he'd noticed things that were only out of the ordinary because they either changed or hadn't been there before: Cherry trees in blossom had replaced the evergreens by the fountain a few times, making him wonder which type were actually supposed to be there. Once he'd seen large iron statues and ornamental pillars instead of garbage cans, while the exact number of benches in a given area had changed several times. (In the latter case, maybe someone had been moving the benches around... although the sudden appearances and disappearances of the heavy-looking pillars and statues were a little hard to explain.)

However, no matter how intense the possible-delusion had been, he'd already gotten used to experiencing them long before he'd snuck out of the sanatorium for the first time. His exposure to phenomena outside had just been a little depressing; it had proven that his (or reality's) problem didn't just exist in the psych building.

Still, what he saw at night (and on odd occasion during the day) hadn't been menacing in any way, so he just accepted it.

While Johnny would spend time exploring the grounds and or venturing into the other buildings, he'd just as often retreat to his usual resting spot: A narrow dirt path on the grass led the way to a series of grassy slopes. Topped with tall leafy trees, the hills were just outside the loose circle of large buildings and the area they enclosed. Sitting atop the highest of the small hills, his back resting against a thick tree trunk, he would absently gaze at the well-lit compound before him.

The lights were bright enough to keep him in plain sight of any passers-by below who might bother to look his way. Usually, a person would casually glance up at him and think nothing of it, likely having mistaken Johnny for an ordinary hospital patient, as opposed to an escapee from the sanatorium building. Since every building on the premises served a different function—within the broad scheme of the health sciences—it would have been difficult for anyone to know which one he'd been staying at, and thus what kind of patient he was.

Meanwhile, Johnny would respond to the rare looks of suspicion from security guards with a grin and a wink.

Not one of those people had chased after him or asked what he was doing, which had always struck him as bizarre. On the far side of the hill, there was a parking lot and, beyond it, the city outside the boundaries of the hospital; no fences or security to impede the completion of his escape. After spending as long as a couple of hours with freedom in his grasp, Johnny would begin to question why he wasn't taking the opportunity to leave for good.

Then he would routinely revisit an old realization:

Escaping was pointless when you had nowhere to retreat, and weren't mentally or emotionally capable of fending for yourself. However, his understanding that obstacle hadn't prevented him from making future attempts to leave the hospital behind. Instead, he would suppress and eventually forget that rather important realization, hoping that some last-minute addition to his plan would suddenly come to him during a future outing. Whatever idea could have made his rejoining society feasible still hadn't come to him, neither during an actual escape attempt nor a practice run.

Maybe that was why nobody bothered to chase after him: Nobody needed to apprehend him and return him to his bed by force, or even make a verbal fuss about his lengthy wanderings outside the psych building. With an absence of options, Johnny was utterly dependant on the hospital and its staff, and he suspected his jailors knew it; they knew his escapades would inevitably end with his return to his room, feeling defeated.

Eventually, he'd decided that he had to find out why nobody talked about his activities. To test his theory, during one of his feigned erratic emotional outbursts, he'd outright bragged about how many times he'd escaped the psych building in Dr. Saunders's presence. Yeah, he'd dreaded being returned to the Hole, but he'd also been desperate to know what the staff knew.

To his dismay, the staff's responses of complacent nods and shrugs had not only confirmed that they'd known about his escapades all along, but also that they'd never taken them seriously. Even Doctor Saunders had appeared largely apathetic towards Johnny's ranting; if anything, his face had betrayed only a trace of amusement.

Johnny, feeling beaten and depressed, once again returned his attention to his present surroundings.

# Chapter 2

DR. SAUNDERS CONTINUED his pacing, now a good twenty minutes after he'd finished bugging everyone with stupid questions. In all that time, he hadn't slowed down or stopped once.

There was a subtle hint of irritation in the doctor's eyes, probably from Johnny's playful griffin remark. Though Johnny hadn't intended it in this instance, Dr. Saunders had probably taken it as a show of artful dissent. As far as he seemed to be concerned, Johnny had just made an underlying accusation, which implied that his confusion was the fault of his caregivers.

Had he consciously aimed to show his disrespect towards Dr. Saunders today by deliberately getting on his nerves (in a way that wouldn't land him in the Hole), Johnny would have been far from satisfied with the doctor's mildly annoyed response. Johnny suddenly realized something else: Even if his making a spectacle of himself had indeed made Dr. Saunders fume, Johnny wouldn't have drawn any satisfaction from it. Right now, his combative form of disruptiveness felt so tiresome and pointless; just like the ritualistic exercises and nonsensical games that Dr. Saunders loved to shove down the patients' throats.

Whenever his sombre mood would set in, as it was doing now, Johnny would reawaken to the fact that nothing worthwhile came out of anything, especially his boisterousness; Dr. Saunders only got better at deflecting Johnny's disruptive air, while none of the patients seemed capable of finding even his sunniest or most over-enthusiastic outbursts amusing or even irritating.

Whether he'd consciously defied or played along with Dr. Saunders's daily condescension and head games, the scheme of things ultimately stayed the same. In hindsight, even the most colourful days fell into a pattern that felt predictable, monotonous.

So, it was just as well that he hadn't consciously planned to be a thorn in Dr. Saunders's side today; facing the futility of trying anything to bring about a lasting, effective change in here would have hit him harder than it already had just now.

If you weren't already insane before being subjected to the never-ending purgatory of this place, Dr. Saunders and his underlings would certainly do their best to ensure that you soon would be.

After what felt like another ten minutes, Dr. Saunders gestured for the patients to follow him, presumably out of the building for the usual after-session walk. Johnny might have sardonically suggested that today must have been a special occasion, since the doctor was going to bother with the menial task of escorting them, instead of one of his underlings; however, he was now too depressed to voice his remark.

Two security guards joined Dr. Saunders at the head of the moving assembly, while two more followed, watching the procession from behind. Since none of the patients present were considered a threat to anyone, the guards usually appeared somewhat lax and really bored.

The session had begun in the early evening, which was unusually late; having lasted for at least a couple of hours, it would be well-past dark and probably lights-out by the time the stroll was over.

The procession stopped a moment in the front lobby, so Dr. Saunders could have a word with the receptionist, who was sitting quietly behind the screen protecting her desk.

Knowing that they'd be casually chatting awhile, Johnny let out an impatient sigh.

His irritated sound drew the attention of Rich, a fellow patient, who turned to give Johnny one of his long, disapproving stares. Standing a couple of inches shorter than Johnny, Rich was a broad-shouldered, big-boned man about the same age as he was—if Johnny actually was somewhere in his mid- to late-twenties.

Johnny was never sure if Rich's humourless, tight-faced expression was an attempt to look intimidating or stern and important; maybe that was just the way his face looked. The thick black frames of his glasses accentuated the uncompromising strictness of his stare, whether or not Rich was directing it towards someone in particular.

Even now, Rich was giving Johnny a look that was haughty, disdainful, and maybe even a little contemptuous. While Johnny couldn't read his mind, Rich definitely appeared to be looking down on him with judgement and condemnation in his eyes.

His first week in the sanatorium, Rich had raved endlessly about his delusions, insisting that everything he said was true. At the time, Johnny himself had been a recent arrival, and had decided to listen passively to whatever the other patients said to him, regretting it in the end. Rich had spent a couple of days talking about how he'd lived among aliens for most of his life, and then had proceeded to talk at length about his having worked for some super-secret government organization. (For a guy who'd said that he had to keep quiet about his role, he'd sure babbled about it a lot.) Within that week, Rich had spun so many yarns that Johnny had lost count of them.

Johnny's personal favourite was Rich's talk about the hospital's top-secret research facility. Supposedly, powerful people were using the property to store something unstable, which a team from another top-secret facility had either created or discovered; something too dangerous for university research centres or military facilities to contain. According to Rich, the hospital had both the means and perfect cover to hide whatever dangerous thing needed containing. The project had presented the risk of catastrophe, so talk of its commencement had drawn the attention of concerned otherworldly observers, long before it had even gotten off the ground.

True, the hospital complex was huge, and, with its abundance of equipment and other resources, medical research did get conducted on the premises. As far as anyone knew, none of the research department's endeavours related to weird meta-physics experiments gone awry or whatever obscurely-defined top-secret thing Rich had been talking about.

Had Rich not kept making such wild claims, jumping from topic to topic like a pathological liar who was hard up for attention, Johnny might have at least entertained a few of his ideas. Rich's last story (except for the "otherworldly observers" part) had more plausibility than the things Johnny himself had experienced here. (Unlike Rich, Johnny knew he'd only sound delusional if he shared any of his unbelievable experiences with anyone, so he refused to do so.)

After about two weeks of being here, Rich had fallen silent like all the other patients, except for Johnny. Johnny had preferred Rich's ridiculous tales to his permanent look of scorn, which had continued for months and was now grating on Johnny's nerves.

"What now?" Johnny asked, snapping the question at his silent antagonist.

Rich said nothing, but continued to stare into Johnny's eyes; a silent act of aggression.

Johnny couldn't help himself:

"You know what? You're a weenie!" he blurted out. "You're king of the weenies!" he added, concluding his counterattack with a long raspberry. Johnny was aware of how childish and ridiculous he looked and sounded, and didn't care. In fact, he defied his self-awareness by flashing Rich a vigorous, manic smile.

His silent antagonist, as he always did these days, said nothing; surprisingly, no one else did, either. Johnny's smile soon faded along with his vigour and the onset of his regressive mode; confronting weirdoes like Rich were getting as tiresome as they were pointless.

Rich turned away, and the entire group suddenly budged forward; Dr. Saunders had just rejoined the front of the procession.

Johnny really had to get away from this place; maybe he'd try escaping again tonight after lights-out. At some point, he was going to have to follow through with his plan to leave this place permanently, even if the outside world would swallow him whole. As awful as that outcome would undoubtedly be, Johnny still preferred it to spending another minute surrounded by these… these… weenies. (That's how he felt for now, anyway.)

As much as he hated to admit it, the fresh air did him good. The remnant of daylight faded into night, and, fortunately, his overactive imagination hadn't acted up at all today—at least, there'd been nothing noticeably out of place.

The stars were unusually clear and bright against the many sources of light pollution down here, which included the many lampposts on the property. Still, there was nothing overwhelmingly weird about the stars, or anything else, really. So far, he had no reason to be deterred from making a break for the city.

As the patients were led back into the psychiatric building, Johnny hoped that his lucky streak would continue all the way to his quarters…

As it turned out, Dr. Saunders hadn't escorted them to an area remotely close to the patients' rooms. Even though Dr. Saunders had said nothing about a change of accommodations tonight, Johnny recognized the door to the gloomy ward, with its uninviting ambience and crappy beds.

No one said anything; Johnny was about to, but, upon entering the large room, he was too startled to speak. A rush of depression hit him the moment he saw black tables where beds used to be, never mind all of the other changes to the ward. Long booth seats ran along the wall to either side of the entrance, offering the only seat for each of the oval tables. Meanwhile, a counter and adjacent bar sat near the back of the room.

It was hard to say if the dimensions of the room had changed. The new décor, including paintings on the walls, could have made the place seem shorter and wider than he'd remembered. The soft amber lighting, radiating from fancy ceiling fixtures, could have contributed to the perceived difference in the room's size as well.

The brown carpeting, wooden baseboards, and beige plaster walls completed the look of a comfy place; specifically a familiar-looking bistro, which was threatening to stir up memories Johnny didn't want to recall.

Horrified that his mind (or the world it was perceiving) was acting up again, he watched as the patients climbed onto the uncomfortable-looking tabletops, before lying on their backs without complaint.

Not wanting to alert Dr. Saunders to his deteriorating grip on reality, Johnny moved towards the nearest unoccupied table. Trying to maintain a casual gait, he probably looked as conspicuously uptight and self-conscious as he felt.

Looking at the reflective surface of the tabletop, he paused to figure out how to best climb atop it without making his confusion about the task obvious.

It was too late:

"What are you doing?" Doctor Saunders asked, sounding irritated and puzzled. He let out a long sigh, as if making a controlled show of weariness from prolonged exasperation.

Then, he continued in an unsettlingly calm voice:

"Haven't we had enough of your foolishness for today? Now hustle onto that table and get some sleep."

A sudden plea to the heavens escaped Johnny's eyes: Why did this have to happen now?

To make matters worse, Johnny had just heard the word "table," which meant that this was going to be one of those nights in which his ears would be conspiring against him alongside his eyes and other senses.

"The hallucinations again?" asked Dr. Saunders with a radical change of tone: There was a twisted fascination in his voice and on his face, which Johnny found a tad disturbing… to put it mildly.

Johnny didn't want to admit it, though he was also reluctant to deny it; it was hard, if not impossible, to hide things from Dr. Saunders. So, Johnny gave him a blank stare, neither confirming nor denying anything.

"Have you been taking your medication?" The question came peppered with an underlying accusation, and threat.

Johnny replied with a quick succession of earnest nods.

"Interesting," Dr. Saunders muttered, looking Johnny over with fascination.

Normally, Johnny would get gawked at like this for a few minutes, and then commanded to perform a few oddball tasks, like raising one hand while touching his nose with the index finger of the other. Then he'd be asked the usual questions about what he was experiencing exactly, while Dr. Saunders or one of his colleagues took notes. If Johnny's day proved to be one of the typically terrible ones, he'd also get a bottle of different meds; Dr. Saunders would insist that the medication was a refill of the same stuff, while forbidding Johnny from disputing the point.

It was late, so, thankfully, Dr. Saunders only approached the table and began patting its surface in the way someone did when encouraging a cat or dog to come to the spot.

The look in the doctor's eyes said it all: "We'll talk about this tomorrow."

Trying not to shudder, Johnny did as his master bid him, awkwardly climbing the tabletop and lying down on his back. Surprisingly, the surface felt a lot like his mattress; as far as mattresses went, it wasn't soft, but it didn't feel anything like a wooden tabletop, either.

Dr. Saunders and his minions departed, the brightness of the bulbs uniformly dimmed to the low level of a nightlight, and the patients were left to get their sleep.

Still lying on his back, Johnny stared straight up at the domed stucco ceiling, which seemed newer than the other changes in here. Feeling without hope and depressed, he couldn't be bothered to give the ceiling— or his table-bed—any more thought.

Like he always did in moments like these, Johnny began to think and semi-selectively remember all sorts of things, hoping they wouldn't stress him out too much...

He thought about how these people hadn't done anything to improve his state of mind over the course of what must have been years. If anything, they seemed determined to keep him here. After all his mischief and shows of defiance, he would have thought that they'd have been glad to give him thorough, consistent, and effective treatment, being eager to see him go.

Getting on everyone's nerves was second nature to Johnny these days, even when he hadn't meant to be bothersome (as far as he could tell consciously).

Lightening the emotional burden of his glum thoughts a moment, Johnny began to recall this one time in particular:

He and a couple of other patients had been all set to leave the hospital grounds, beginning a supervised daytrip to a nearby park. The four of them—including the nurse—had just reached the front of the main hospital building, when Johnny had noticed a large banner posted over the entrance of the Emergency Ward:

"Visit Our New Children's Emergency Room: Coming Soon!"

Unable to keep his mouth shut, he'd tugged on the nurse's sleeve while pointing at the sign:

"Don't they mean they're downsizing the hospital and no longer admitting adult patients?" he'd asked innocuously.

"Never mind about that, Johnny; it's a beautiful day and we're going to go out for a while. Why don't we just enjoy the weather?"

"It just seems like such horsy-poop," he'd said, unable to take his eyes off the sign while frowning at it suspiciously. "You know, these people making like they're bringing something new and improved, with all the colourful lettering and all that... when really they're just taking something away."

The nurse had shrugged, before sighing with a look of impatience.

"It just seems like a bit of a slap in the face, if you ask me; pretending that this wonderful thing is coming, when they're really more or less happily advertising that they're going to stop admitting patients over seventeen."

"Well, no one did ask you, Johnny. Now, are you finished with your little social commentary?"

"Not really," he'd replied casually. "I'm also wondering how the health sciences company running all the local hospitals can justify asking people for donations when they're pulling scams like this. I'm not sure where I'd heard about it, but isn't there some telemarketing campaign going on right about now?"

She hadn't answered to confirm or deny what Johnny had briefly overheard among the hospital staff when he'd been on one of his strolls outside the psychiatric building.

"Well, if there is canvassing for donations on top of short-ending and misleading the public, there's certainly something to be said about that: 'Please give us your money on top of your tax dollars, so we can turn you away from the nearest hospital, when every minute counts, because your eighteenth birthday was last week,' is pretty nervy, isn't it?"

If there had been an explanation for what seemed misleading, maybe even downright crooked, it had become clear that this nurse wasn't going to give it.

In hindsight, Johnny supposed that she probably didn't know or care enough to think about the issue. It was hard to say whether or not she had set out to unconditionally defend tacky administrative decisions… like posting signs that came off as dishonest and added insult to the injury of rejected would-be patients.

Even so, Johnny didn't really understand why she'd been so moody with him when he brought up the subject (or any subject at all really). A few—though not all—of the staff were like that, though; if you were a mental patient, then they assumed that you had nothing to say worth discussing… even if the point you made had some merit, and you'd gone out of your way to express it articulately.

Oh well.

As the four of them had continued on their way, the nurse had kept her eye on Johnny while doing her best to keep her distance from him. While she wasn't what one could call a licensed therapist, she hadn't hesitated to share her personal words of wisdom through casual conversation… at least, with the other two who hadn't ticked her off. Of course, they hadn't said anything to her, or to anyone.

Once they'd reached the grass field of the park, she'd made the most significant comment of the day, though it hadn't been significant in the way she'd probably intended:

"Personally, I believe it's important to live life to the fullest. We should treat every moment like it's our last."

Impulsively, Johnny had shrieked and broken out into an aimless run throughout the field, just before dropping into a ball on the grass. Although he'd kept his eyes tightly shut and his ears firmly plugged with his fingers, he'd still heard the nurse yelling at him with exasperation in her voice:

"What you doing?" she'd demanded.

Unplugging his ears and then opening his eyes, he'd lifted his head off the ground to answer:

"Living like it's my last moment on Earth," he'd said hurriedly, his voice conveying tension and panic. Then, he'd quickly resumed his position, concealing his eyes and ears from an impending cataclysm.

(Even at the time, he hadn't been sure if he'd really felt the anxiety or not.)

"It's just a figure of speech!" the nurse had replied irritably.

The remark had made the anxiety—real, imagined, or self-induced— dissipate instantly. After unplugging his ears and opening his eyes again, he'd given her a frown of confusion and light annoyance.

"How so?" he'd asked, genuinely failing to understand what she'd meant. "Either you live like you're about to meet your maker within seconds or you don't. I mean, I'm not going to plan for tomorrow if there isn't going to be one, right? Why would I make any plans at all; take a course, start a big project, or do anything that involves investing time if none of it is going to come close to fruition?"

"Getting smart-mouthed are we?"

In truth, Johnny wasn't really sure if his intention had been to ridicule her remark or if he had genuinely decided to put the old cliché to the test, while letting his imagination get the better of him.

In any case, his outburst had been the reason the trip had ended early. Dr. Saunders had been notified of Johnny's conduct shortly thereafter, and Johnny had found himself locked inside his quarters for the rest of the day.

Thoughts of that misadventure brought another one to mind. Happening well after the shortened day trip, the incident had made Dr. Saunders the most visibly furious with Johnny:

It had started with a visit from the crew of a local news station. Wandering near the doctor's office—after having snuck out of his room for one of his usual strolls—Johnny had overheard the head of the psychiatric hospital making some sanctimonious, self-congratulatory spiel to the reporter interviewing him. From what Johnny had been able to tell, they'd been discussing the stigma of mental illness.

"It is regrettable and shameful that people tend to regard those suffering from mental illness with disdain, and as if they are in some way inherently dangerous."

Contrary to what he'd just said, Dr. Saunders couldn't care less about the patients under the care of his staff; his intimating otherwise had made Johnny want to puke.

Johnny also remembered how Dr. Saunders had previously come up in the news because of his vocal motion to grant one of the particularly violent patients in the high-security wing freedom. Basically, he'd said that the patient wouldn't pose a threat, "so long as he continued to take his medication."

The thing was, that violent patient hadn't taken his meds the first time around, which was why he'd ended up doing something criminal in the first place; something that would have gotten him the death penalty in some places.

After Johnny had rushed up to the reporter as she'd emerged from the office—surprising both her and Dr. Saunders—he'd been quick to blurt out his own opinion:

"That stigma is just as much the fault of that man, you know," he'd said to her, repeatedly pointing at Dr. Saunders as though he were poking at the air in front of him.

Johnny had ignored Dr. Saunders's demand to know what he was doing out of his room, while, surprisingly, the reporter was interested in what Johnny had to say. In the span of time between Dr. Saunders calling security and their arrival to cart him off, Johnny had managed to get a few of his voiced thoughts on camera:

"You can't have it both ways and say, 'Oh, that guy viciously killed someone because he's mentally ill,' and then say, 'Well, because he's mentally ill, that changes what happened; he's not criminally responsible so we'll just throw a few pills at him and say he's free to go whenever he looks stable enough.'

"The stated reason for a criminal act and the defence used to dismiss the charge are the same thing; doesn't that seem a little messed up to you? It doesn't change what happened or how threatened society is."

Johnny, running out of time, hadn't waited for the reporter to respond:

"Besides, it makes the rest of us look bad. Yeah, there's prejudice out there in some cases, but I can't honestly say I'd blame a person for feeling uneasy if I were given a license to kill… on account of my being here and all."

The reporter had seemed a little nervous when he'd said that. Still, he continued hurriedly:

"Besides, of course people are going to get tetchy if people like Saunders try to shift the onus of proof on everyone else to show that the unsupervised patient is likely to do harm again. How about Saunders accepts the burden of proof and demonstrates irrefutable evidence that his violent patient won't harm anyone ever again?

"Saunders wants to give special privileges to certain people, which is really where a lot of the apprehension and danger comes from."

"Why do you think Dr. Saunders would do something like that?" she'd asked, looking as though she were humouring him (possibly stalling while waiting for the security guys to show up). She'd also sounded a little like a counsellor; one of the ones who'd imply that you only felt a certain way about something, and that your impression was likely false.

Johnny had answered her anyway:

"Hubris," he'd said, voicing his theory matter-of-factly. "He'll throw other people under the bus to get his way while stubbornly trying to prove some point… if I were to guess, in my humble opinion," he'd concluded, offering a smile and courteous bow… just a second before he was grabbed by either arm and hauled out of her presence.

"Nice talking to you!" he'd managed to call out to her.

She'd given him an awkward smile while Dr. Saunders had simply scowled at him, just before Johnny had been dragged completely out of their view.

He wasn't sure if his interjection (which arguably had involved ambushing the reporter) had made it to the news or not, but the doctor had been cranky enough to send him to the Hole for an indefinite period of time, which had felt like forever.

Whether or not anyone else saw it, Johnny knew Dr. Saunders was full of it whenever he talked about helping people, reducing stigmas, or doing good in general. Beyond trying to look virtuous, as though the doctor were trying to win a "Citizen of the Year" award or something, his sententious, sanctimonious, self-righteous façade had nothing behind it, except possibly a desire to appear noble, to get recognition.

Well, maybe Johnny didn't "know" it for sure, but the good of others seemed to be a distant priority for Dr. Saunders, whether or not enhancing his image and boosting his ego came first. Johnny had to admit that at least half of Dr. Saunders's behaviour probably wasn't considered normal or acceptable for even the biggest quacks and egomaniacs in his field. (Unfortunately, given Johnny's position, he doubted anyone—who wasn't complicit in the weird goings-on here—would believe his account; the statement would just get relayed back to Dr. Saunders.)

The most mean-spiritedly depicted stereotypes of arrogant, high-standing professionals and fake humanitarians (of those Johnny knew about) had nothing on Dr. Saunders.

One thing was for sure, if he were such a big humanitarian, Dr. Saunders wouldn't threaten or "discipline" the patients who weren't actually dangerous; he'd sporadically sent Johnny to his quarters without supper for something as little as giving him the raspberry, or to the Hole with far less reason.

Johnny already had general knowledge of high-standing hypocritical and arrogant jerks like Dr. Saunders, since there were abusive and negligent caregivers of all kinds. However, his having a punishment like the Hole at his disposal was not only another radical deviation from the standard tools of corrupt figures; it was also unnatural, in the otherworldly sense.

Then there were those other bizarre and dreamlike things here, popping up to startle him from time to time as if to aid Dr. Saunders's desire to keep Johnny mad. As much as Johnny had routinely tried to, he couldn't dismiss them as mere hallucinations. (Too often, he'd been left wondering if he was living in an actual nightmare or if he was as crazy as people said.)

Johnny paused his train of thought to shiver a little before pulling it back to the topic of Dr. Saunders.

Aside from Dr. Saunders's creepy and extraordinarily sinister behaviour towards Johnny, there was another aspect of hypocrisy to Dr. Saunders's melodramatic pontificating about human dignity, condemning bigotry while pretending to care about his patients:

The doctor certainly didn't condemn the seemingly-ordinary (and understandable) precautions those running the hospital had taken, as much as he liked decrying stigmas to the point of redundancy. For one thing, he'd always seemed to be fine with the protective window, which shielded the reception desk.

If there was nothing to be cautious about from anyone, then why was it there?

That reception area wasn't just for the high-security wing; it was for the whole psych hospital.

Yup; Dr. Saunders sure liked to fluctuate between his extremes. Out of one side of his mouth, the guy couldn't stop implicitly congratulating himself as he'd condemn the public's alleged attitude towards mental illness, in order to shame concerned citizens whenever they worried about the release of violent, criminally-insane offenders. To the public, with pretences of moral superiority, he'd acted like all worries about such things under any circumstances were detestable. (Gee, Johnny thought sardonically, if the public pleaded insanity, would Dr. Saunders's tune change; would he then decide that condemning concerned citizens would be harsh and inappropriate of him?)

Meanwhile, the other side of his mouth, through his actions, yielded far more than just the normal precautionary measures of protective windows and security:

Again, while Johnny could list a few other things, the Hole came to mind.

Whenever he'd thought about the Hole, Johnny would keep his mouth shut. He wouldn't have even made light jokes about things like the security screen protecting the receptionist behind her desk.

Sure, he'd still thought about making the odd cheesy wisecrack to the receptionist; like maybe asking her if she was keeping a lot of cash under her desk, or if she thought this was a different part of the hospital and was worried about contamination.

Since she was frowny-faced and tended to talk down towards people, he really had to hold his tongue. Instead of actually saying anything, he always imagined asking her snide questions, brimming with mock suspicion:

"Say, you wouldn't be getting nasty and disdainful because you're behind that window, now would you? You know, taking advantage of your safety barrier by making faces at us, since you're certain that nobody could just put a fist-sized hole in that window and quickly pull you towards the glass by your collar?"

No; that definitely would have been a bad idea. While he tried not to remember past appointments with even ordinary physicians (though he must have had a physical at some point in his life), he was pretty darn sure that questions like that would have gotten him thrown out of even the most laidback medical practice.

He'd definitely refrained from the idea of using a glasscutter to make a hole in the pane, so he could give the receptionist a friendly poke... just to reassure her that he wasn't a bad guy.

(Of course, he wasn't really sure how he could pull off such a thing, anyway.)

While he'd gotten better at holding back from doing things that were reckless and stupid (which sometimes made sense at the time and sometimes didn't at all), the trouble was that he'd still forget himself and about the Hole at least fifty-percent of the time. Whenever he did sporadically overlook those rather important things, he'd usually say or do something hasty and flippant in that childishly regressive sort of way.

A spell of acting with extreme silliness would come and go, and only after it had passed would he then realize just how silly his behaviour had been. Usually, that realization would come to him while he was in his quarters, during a period of quiet self-reflection.

He supposed there were worse things than the Hole; or that's what he would keep telling himself while he was in it. There was, after all, the rest of this hospital, and the conventional kinds of threats that were at least just as dangerous, even if they were less spooky.

While he couldn't say what the prevailing state of the main hospital was for sure, he'd overheard things said among the staff and interns that had given him a really nasty impression of it. During one of his unscheduled and unsupervised walks through the main hospital, he'd overheard one particularly memorable conversation, which had taken place between what looked like two interns.

The pair had been laughing about a certain then-recent mix-up: A patient had "accidentally" been given a tracheotomy instead of the procedure he'd actually been scheduled to receive.

The only thing more unsettling than the mix-up itself was these people's unsympathetic amusement about it, their lack of conscience in treating the issue as though it were a casual silly anecdote. Johnny had found their talk about an accidental tracheotomy horrifying enough as it was, even without their finding it so funny or having such an uncaring and unapologetic attitude towards betraying their patients.

He'd been so shocked that he hadn't quite taken in the detail of what the correct operation should have been: These were the professionals to whom people entrusted their lives?

Those were the "ordinary" patients getting harmed, too; the kind who had the credibility in others' eyes to make complaints that would be taken seriously.

Still the staff here didn't care, even out of selfishly wanting to preserve their careers, which was odd. (Maybe they were just cocky, thinking nothing ever would come of their actions.)

Yikes.

Johnny really hoped he didn't get sick or physically injured in here, and end up having to rely on the rest of the hospital to fix him up. After ruining his life, they'd probably skip giving him the usual lip-service apology before snickering about their negligence behind his back.

Then again, between Dr. Saunders and the other frightening things about the sanatorium specifically, Johnny had the feeling that if anything did eventually happen to him, he wouldn't make it out of the psych building (or wherever the Hole was). The likelihood of that impression certainly made worrying about the rest of the hospital moot.

On a part-time basis, Johnny had reluctantly acknowledged the notion that his memories of being a patient here might not have been accurate, thanks to the insistence of Dr. Saunders. However, Johnny trusted him the least of all the staff here, so the idea never really stuck.

He still couldn't get over it: Whether listening to Dr. Saunders with a group of patients or alone, Johnny had been told over and over again that whatever he'd thought he'd remembered even a week beforehand had been completely wrong. Yet, the only memories Johnny had remained consistent, and they deviated quite far from the ever-changing history that Dr. Saunders routinely told him to accept.

Dr. Saunders had at least agreed with Johnny that his memories of their arguments were real. Johnny would accuse Dr. Saunders of trying to drive him crazier than he already was by making him question his ability to remember things accurately, then the two would get into a heated yelling session over the subject, and then Johnny would find himself poked with a needle, sedated, and sent to the Hole.

Between fear of punishment and listening to well-respected professionals telling him that he couldn't trust his perception of reality, Johnny had still felt tempted to disbelieve what he thought he knew from time to time. Eventually, he'd resume trusting himself and distrusting the likes of Dr. Saunders, a little more resentful after each cycle of psychological abuse.

Nowadays, Johnny usually kept his real feelings to himself; he knew Dr. Saunders was a liar, but he'd say nothing of it while listening to the latest yarn about Johnny's history.

Johnny wondered if Dr. Saunders suspected that Johnny was still refusing to buy whatever he was told, or if Dr. Saunders even cared. After all, Johnny had no choice but to take the new drugs he'd been given upon receiving the latest revised diagnosis.

Of course, according to Dr. Saunders, the diagnosis had always been consistent, and Johnny had only imagined the change of pills, the increase of being poked with needles, and the reason why he was imprisoned here.

Having a drug-addled brain, from pills and injections he couldn't name, had probably contributed to Johnny's limited willingness to believe what Dr. Saunders had told him for a time. Whether he'd built a partial resistance to those drugs or his willpower had eventually negated some of their effects, they weren't burying the contents of his mind anymore.

He supposed he'd found a little consolation in the fact that the effort he'd made to forget his life before coming here had been simplified with the meds. Then again, dealing with the strain to control what and how much of it he wanted to remember was better than becoming an empty slate who could be convinced to accept false memories while forgetting what he needed to remember.

How did it all begin, anyway?

Oh yeah…

# Chapter 3

EVEN AT THIS very moment, though he still hesitated to do it, Johnny could manage to take a quick peek at his past; he just had to reach back far enough to reassure himself that he'd come to this hospital voluntarily. He'd had acute anxiety problems, arguably a nervous breakdown; at least, that was the story both Johnny's boss and a psychiatrist had given him, just before they'd sent him to this place.

He needed to keep that in mind, though he also needed to refrain from thinking about it.

"Why? Because," he mentally reminded himself, "My past is too stressful to face."

For the first few weeks of Johnny's stay, Dr. Saunders had seconded the diagnosis he'd already been given, which was fine... though he hadn't been sure why he'd needed the injections to keep him tranquilized, or if his taking pills alongside the injections (or at all) was a good idea.

At the time, Johnny had trusted Dr. Saunders enough to obey his instructions and accept the mysterious contents of the unmarked bottle, though he had felt a little strange about taking medication directly from the psychiatrist without a formal prescription. He'd asked if they were antidepressants, and Dr. Saunders had answered him with a hint of a smile and cock of his head; Johnny had forced himself to take that as a yes, even if it was a shifty one.

So, he'd downed one of the white pills each day for a couple of weeks. Between the sedatives and the desperate urge he'd had to listen to the doctor, Johnny hadn't pressed him to be forthcoming about what he was taking. Still, he'd had a problem with the fact that Dr. Saunders wouldn't even tell Johnny the actual name of the medication, or if there were any side effects.

The trouble had started—or become apparent—the moment Johnny had summoned the courage to confront Dr. Saunders about his evasiveness, after Johnny's meekly-asked questions had been ignored several times. As politely as he could, he'd expressed his need to know just what type of antidepressants he'd been taking, assuming they really were antidepressants.

That had been the first time Dr. Saunders had told him that Johnny needed to calm down, with the air of a threat in his voice. After Johnny had backed off, Dr. Saunders gave him another unmarked bottle, filled with translucent capsules filled with yellow powder. Calmly reciting a long name Johnny couldn't remember and wouldn't have been able to pronounce, Dr. Saunders had then told him that it was to treat his bi-polar disorder.

Had Johnny not already been given a different diagnosis, he would have been fine with that; the issue was nothing to be ashamed of, though it had seemed a little odd to be put in a hospital for it. He'd told Dr. Saunders as much, calmly and politely, and also that he'd noticed the meds were different from what he'd been given last time.

Maybe he'd had Johnny confused with a different patient?

Shaking his head with a disparaging look, Dr. Saunders had firmly insisted that Johnny had been the one who was mistaken, and that he'd have to learn to control his temper. Shocked and disbelieving, he hadn't had the time to react to the sudden appearance of two large men, who'd hauled Johnny away to the Hole for the first time. (Dr. Saunders still had the gall to call the place the "Quiet Room.")

That first time had also been the most memorable. Johnny supposed he was going to have to relive a bit of it sooner or later:

Since he hadn't had a clue of what they'd had in store for him, he'd been too confused to struggle or protest as the two silent thugs had dragged him out of Dr. Saunders's office. Although he'd offered no resistance, he'd felt something sharp aggressively stab its way into his neck, robbing him of consciousness.

After recovering from the heaviest sedation he'd experienced in the sanatorium (up until that point), he'd found himself lying on his back in darkness. His body had been resting atop a lopsided mattress on a broken bed frame. For whatever reason, someone had loosely wrapped his body in long white bandages from the neck down.

Lifting his head and looking around, he'd realized that, even without a light source of any kind, his eyes had been able to make out the dimensions of the room, as well as most of the objects in it. While he'd found that a bit strange, he'd had no problem with it.

The floor in there was so perfectly black that, initially, he hadn't been sure that there was one. In the absence of light, the ceiling and walls had appeared as a soft blurry mix of black, blue-blacks, and blue-greys; had the lights been on, he doubted he'd have seen walls that were uniformly white... or clean... or in good repair.

He'd been left alone in what had struck him as an unusually small and seemingly abandoned hospital room, its floor stretching no more than ten feet from back to front and twelve feet across.

Lots of junk had been piled and strewn about the room, either in the middle of the floor or carelessly stacked near the walls. From what he could tell, it had all been hospital equipment, probably old and disused for quite some time:

He'd recognized a dialysis machine, a few electrocardiogram machines, and other patient-monitoring devices with dials and screens. There'd been canisters and ventilators—probably for anaesthesia— defibrillators, and electrosurgical units. To his disgust there'd also been bedpans and syringes littering areas of the floor, as well as broken glass and other sharp-looking objects... not to mention heaps of discarded bandages, rags, and large cotton balls. Scalpels and other small surgical tools, probably rusty and unclean, had been resting atop a nearby wheelie tray.

By the end of his inspection from the bed, the room had seemed to be little more than a large broom closet. It had struck him as a place where some lazy doctor had decided to store his outdated, possibly broken equipment and dispose of his garbage.

To his disconcertment, there'd been a crumpled intravenous bag on a stand next to him. The thick liquid inside had filled him with dread, or at least until he'd realized that neither of his arms had been hooked into the IV.

Johnny had been startled at the sudden sight of a gentle blue light entering the room. Spilling in through a barred window on the left wall, its source had been too blue to be moonlight. While he'd been sure that the light entering the window had been artificially generated, he had no idea if it was coming from outdoors.

At first, Johnny had imagined an unconventional surgical light or lamp as the source. Its harshly bright centre, looking a couple of feet wide, had been drifting a little from side to side. He hadn't been able to see or hear any sign of a person behind that window, holding or directing a big lantern, which he'd found a little spooky.

He'd also seen what looked like a small keypad on the wall between the window and the floor; he didn't know what it was doing there or what it was supposed to unlock.

For a little while, fear had paralyzed Johnny, keeping him firmly on the mattress. Even after he'd started to hear things, he hadn't moved. The unintelligible mutters, faint whispers, and low groans had sounded just inches away from his ears.

He'd even remained frozen when he'd started to see vaguely-humanoid shadows appearing on the softly-illuminated walls. The shadows had cycled through sweeping into his field of vision from the corner of his eye, lingering a few seconds while making subtle movements, and then quickly darting away. None of the shapes had any source he could pinpoint, though his staying still had limited his ability to check thoroughly.

Eventually, all the activity had stopped, at which point Johnny had found his nerve to do something. He'd started by hurriedly pulling off the bandages and then carefully getting off the mattress, making sure that his slippers didn't come into contact with anything but empty space on the floor. Even with the blue light still emanating through the bars of the window, it had been hard to see the open doorway on the opposite wall to his right.

He'd exited the room cautiously, only to be startled by the sudden flicker of fluorescent lights above. They'd lit up a narrow off-white hallway lined with doorways, most of them without actual doors. His eyes had caught sight of heaps of dirty-looking rags littering the black rubber matting, which covered the floor.

Then, after a couple of seconds, the bulbs in the ceiling had gone dead again; soon after, they'd begun to flicker sporadically, like intermittent flashes of lightening. As unnerving as he'd found that flickering, it had at least made seeing where he was going possible. Inching forward down the passage, he'd kept each hand on either wall, and had stopped during each succession of flashes to take a good look around. As bright as it was, the sudden bursts of light hadn't permeated the threshold of any of the doorways; the openings had looked solid in their blackness.

Yet, when he'd braved peering through a couple of them, he'd see small rooms nearly identical to the one in which he'd awakened. Eerily enough, he'd even made out a barred window on the far side of each room, with blue light spilling between the bars.

Johnny had wandered for what had felt like an hour, carefully avoiding the rags, hoping they didn't constitute a biohazard. He'd noticed that the hallway didn't have right angles or junctions; rather, he'd been walking along gentle curves, as if travelling down the innards of a snake, which periodically forked into two or more passages. Unsure if he'd been imagining it or not, Johnny could have sworn that he'd been travelling on a decline.

He'd kept thinking to himself: Wherever he was, this place was deserted. So, everyone (except for those who'd put him here) had probably forgotten about it. Whether it was an abandoned section of the hospital or a secluded building that was miles away from the property, no one would ever find him here (no one he'd want to meet, anyway).

It had felt like two hours when he'd finally reached what had looked like an unmarked exit; a windowed door with a stairwell beyond. Though the stairs had only been visible under the irregularly flickering lights, Johnny had carefully descended them all the same. The only other door inside the stairwell had been at the bottommost landing.

His newfound hope had been deflated as quickly as it had been stirred; he'd found himself entering a hallway identical to the one he'd only thought he'd escaped.

Without clocks, Johnny had no idea how long he'd been trapped in the maze. After a long stretch of anxiously pacing and dolefully lingering in the hallway, desperation had taken a hold of Johnny and he'd begun to search the rooms frantically but fruitlessly.

The sounds of voices had returned, following him into the hallway. They'd also gotten quite loud. When they hadn't been shrieking or roaring from far ahead or behind, they'd been barking or hissing in his ears.

In hindsight, he wasn't sure if that had been before or after he'd started seeing shadows flying along the walls whenever the lights flickered to life. Misshapen figures had also begun manifesting on the edge of his field of vision; their appearances had been too fleeting and too blurry for him to see any of the apparitions clearly.

No one had come to check up on him, even after he'd screamed and begged to be let out.

Eventually, an inner voice had told him to go to sleep. While he couldn't recall obeying it, he did remember waking up back in his quarters.

Dr. Saunders had been waiting by his bedside with an infuriatingly self-satisfied look on his face.

"Perhaps following Doctor's Orders isn't so unreasonable after all," he'd remarked, mocking Johnny with a hint of a cheery smile.

That nightmare had indeed kept Johnny quiet for a time. There'd actually been quite a long phase where he'd said nothing, even when he'd still wanted to emphasize that he'd come here voluntarily and should have been allowed to leave any time he wanted to.

Johnny had hated every second of it, but he'd cooperatively sat through the long-winded spiels about his having a different mental ailment every few weeks, straining to ignore the fact that the medication he'd receive every time was visibly different.

Johnny couldn't even remember all the variations of acute anxiety or personality disorders he'd been told he had. Dr. Saunders had even cycled through a few of them a couple of times. One day he'd say that Johnny had been suffering from intense anxiety or some phobia or another. Then, about a month or so later, he'd say that Johnny had been suffering from delusions, perhaps from an offshoot of some schizotypal issue. Not long after that, he would insist that Johnny was in here because he had some rare form of dementia.

Before going back to diagnosing Johnny with an anxiety disorder again, and beginning the cycle anew, he would introduce a new bizarre claim or two: One day, Johnny would be told that his brain had been irreparably damaged due to prolonged drug use (even though Johnny was sure that he'd never even dabbled in such things). The next, he would be informed that he had some other obscure personality disorder, which had supposedly made it impossible for Johnny to function in the outside world.

Although Johnny hadn't said anything, Dr. Saunders would insist that, yes, his diagnosis had always been the same, and that Johnny had always been given the same pills (or capsules).

He must have gotten sick of Johnny's semi-submissive silence. No longer willing to talk about anything on his mind, since he'd feared punishment for expressing his thoughts, Johnny had stopped saying anything. Instead, he'd only shrugged in response to whatever question Dr. Saunders would ask him. Eventually, Dr. Saunders had decided that Johnny was being passive-aggressively uncooperative, and that drastic measures needed to be taken.

That occasion had marked Johnny's second trip to the Hole, which had been nearly identical to the first; and just like every trip after. Still,

Johnny had never gotten used to it.

From then on, life was a blur of ever-changing diagnoses, pills he would take (or get sent to the Hole for refusing to take), and group sessions with people who didn't talk much.

Johnny wasn't sure when his manic, carefree fits had started… They certainly hadn't started before Dr. Saunders had called him a manic-depressive at least a couple of times. In those modes, Johnny still dreaded the Hole, but had still thought less about being sent to it. Maybe a part of him figured that no matter what he did, he'd always be sent back anyway.

In spite of his hatred of the "Quiet Room," his love of defying Dr. Saunders would still take hold whether he liked it or not. Embracing the fleeting sense of invincibility during his giddiest moments, fed up with feeling terrified of further punishments, he would all but dare the creep to go ahead and punish him.

He'd taken to outright mocking Dr. Saunders after getting a new diagnosis, whether it had been completely new or one he had been given before. It was around that time when Johnny had finally remembered that he wasn't supposed to be here against his will; he'd made a point of reminding Dr. Saunders of the fact.

Now, he wasn't sure if Dr. Saunders's specific diagnosis of the month had already been decided before Johnny had opened his mouth; or, if it had been decided as a response to Johnny's insistence that he wasn't a prisoner.

According to Dr. Saunders, Johnny had been suffering from psychotic episodes due to a rare form of schizophrenia. Johnny still didn't know much about the disorder, whether or not there were really different forms of it, rare or otherwise. Dr. Saunders hadn't even bothered to name the specific disorder, which had only told Johnny that this man had lost interest in trying to sound convincing.

So, in addition to being told that the meds in the latest mystery bottle had always been an antipsychotic, Johnny had also been expected to believe that he hadn't come to the hospital voluntarily.

In fact, Dr. Saunders had told Johnny that he'd been deemed a possible danger to himself and others.

"If that's true, then why am I not in the high-security wing, Mr. Smartypants?" Johnny had asked, on the brink of giving Dr. Saunders one of his raspberries.

His answer had been brief, dismissive, and kind of lazy:

"You don't pose that much of a threat; it's really more for your own safety than anyone else's. The risk-factor towards others in your case is rather remote."

Ah, the "It's for your own good" cliché. When it came from someone like Dr. Saunders, sounding as insincere as it did, it really was just that: A cliché.

He'd gone on, looking indifferent to Johnny's unwillingness to believe him:

"You were brought here because you'd refused a court order to take your medication. Don't you remember that the order had been an alternative to your being 'imprisoned' here, after your episodes had finally landed you in trouble?"

No, actually Johnny hadn't… and he still didn't.

All he remembered (as much as he hated remembering anything) was the culmination of toxicity in his social and professional environments, dealing with people whose behaviour bore a striking resemblance to Dr. Saunders's.

If he thought about each situation, a torrent of considerations would ensue. Then, he'd find himself pulled into the ghost of that confrontation. After that, he'd find himself reliving a vivid exchange with someone loathsome, while his mind heightened the unpleasantness of his or her toxicity. Thinking about anything that reminded him of his life outside the hospital would bring back those ugly experiences, usually more than one at a time.

He'd relive an ugly instance as it had happened, then his mind would add to it. His psyche had a way of anticipating and mentally realizing every twisted response people could possibly use, which would serve to justify whatever deceptive or nefarious thing they'd done, or were ready to do.

However, according to Dr. Saunders, Johnny had been brought here because he'd been barking at people on the sidewalk, in the park, and through the windows of cars and shops. He'd even walked out in front of a few oncoming vehicles in the street, pointing and screaming gibberish at them… after having harassed people in ways that the doctor wouldn't specify.

He'd been brought before a judge and told that, if he didn't want to be put in an institution or prison for his many misdemeanours, then he'd have to take his antipsychotic medication. Johnny had agreed to the terms, but then broke them; within a couple of weeks, he was back to causing mischief, which was what had led to his being brought here.

"Now, do you think that the judge was being too harsh?" Dr. Saunders had asked.

Johnny had thought about that a moment; if a person did something that was dangerous and illegal, something did have to be done about it. After causing so much trouble, only an idiot would suggest that it was somehow oppressive and unreasonable to be expected to take the meds he should have been taking in the first place. (Yeah, there were some people like that, he supposed.)

If anything, it was merciful to get let off with a warning, after being ordered to take responsibility for your actions… especially when others would normally get sent straight to jail in the same situation. In fact, if the person had actually posed a threat to people, some might have argued that getting an order to take prescribed meds was perhaps a little too generous.

As for Johnny, he hadn't committed any such crime, he hadn't been brought before a judge, and—before coming to the sanatorium—he hadn't had any prescribed medication to ditch taking.

"No," Johnny had eventually replied. "It's not 'too harsh'; I just don't believe a word you say. There'd been trouble at work, and I… I…"

Dr. Saunders's familiar look of quiet displeasure had stopped Johnny's painful attempt to recount the incident; that crucial moment he'd reached his breaking point in the outside world, which had led to an appointment with a psychiatrist. Before Dr. Saunders had suggested otherwise, the Hole had been the only place where Johnny had seen, heard, and felt things that he would have been somewhat willing to accept as delusions.

After that conversation (and his then-latest trip to the Hole immediately thereafter), he'd begun to have hallucinations outside the Hole. His spells of seeing and hearing things, which he was sure couldn't have been real, had no longer been restricted to any place. It had been as though the world had taken to adjusting itself to fit Dr. Saunders's diagnosis. Johnny never did shake the feeling that reality was in cahoots with his nemesis... though he grudgingly had to admit that the thought of it did sound a little crazy.

Even now, Johnny was sure of what he remembered about his life before getting allegedly committed. In fact, he often had to wrestle with his mind in order to stop it from remembering. Also, he could tell the difference between memories and imaginings, and, on top of that, he was pretty sure that he knew a solid and real object from an illusionary one.

While trying to figure out just what was going on here, Johnny didn't care for any of the possibilities that came to mind. He couldn't rightly form a belief based on what he wanted to be true, but that didn't stop him from hoping that there was a palatable explanation he hadn't thought of. The only ideas that came to mind were terrifying...

The first possibility: His sanity was so far gone that his memory and his senses were in shambles, leaving him at the mercy of Dr. Saunders, who could claim that his abusive tendencies were all in Johnny's head. The worst part of that scenario was, that Johnny wouldn't be able to reliably test or confirm the difference between fact and fiction in his world. If his mental state made the ability to make discernments impossible, he might have imagined some of the abuse, all of it, or none of it.

The second possibility Johnny could think of entailed something so frightening that he sometimes preferred the idea of having psychotic delusions: If reality in the hospital compound was actually afflicted with some sort of unnatural phenomenon, then everything he thought he knew about how reality worked was wrong. If this place was as unnatural as it had often seemed, everything he understood to be true about the world went right out the window; the laws of physics weren't universal, and this place might not have been a hospital at all. Maybe whatever was causing strange things to happen was also directly rewiring his mind—his memories and perception—from the inside… That would mean that, while he really did have an illness, a malevolent and artificial something was causing it.

Johnny wasn't sure if his mind could really handle that last idea without acquiring a little insanity… the kind of paradoxical craziness that was a perfectly normal reaction to experiencing something unthinkable.

That brought his mind to a third possibility: That he was both delusional and in a place filled with freaky things that were real. If that were true, then there would be no hope of telling the difference between having a delusion and experiencing a real event that defied the orthodox understanding of the natural world. Unable to trust his mind and senses to protect him, he'd be rendered completely defenceless.

While sometimes downplaying the utter weirdness of events, Johnny had also tried to convince himself that there was a reasonable explanation for that weirdness. Instead of committing to any one perception of what was going on here, he'd forced any feelings of certainty about his situation from his mind. After deciding to wait and see what the future would reveal, he'd been surprised to find himself quickly adjusting to the phenomena, whatever their cause.

From then on, he would fluctuate between writing them off as illusions, acting as though his senses were playing tricks on him, and, when that became too ridiculous, letting his mind float towards the idea that there was something objectively weird about this place. Whenever he considered that the phenomena might not have been hallucinations, he would also keep in mind that maybe their cause wasn't as spooky as he had the inclination to think… so he wouldn't panic.

Meanwhile, it was pointless going to the other patients for a second opinion on what they should have witnessed as well. He would have had better luck finding out what they had to say about Dr. Saunders, which was a futile effort. They were useless, often reminding Johnny of extras on a movie set. None of them would or could speak to anyone but Dr. Saunders and his staff. Even then, their words were usually only brief muttered responses to whatever the doctor and his underlings had said to them. He imagined a pack of well-trained dogs barking on command promptly and meekly.

So, Johnny remained alone, forced to rely on a mind that possibly wasn't reliable.

Johnny had also found himself caught up in yet another cycle of going back and forth, which had never ceased; from a state of entertaining what Dr. Saunders had said (after being subjected to head games and drugs) to one of arguing with the jerk. He wasn't sure when he'd first noticed this cycle, and how it paralleled his other transitions… Specifically, there was his shift from remaining quietly cooperative (or pretending to be) to being obnoxiously disruptive. There was also his tendency to go from being serious and intensely contemplative (to the point of emotional exhaustion) to being impulsive, giddy, and childlike.

As if giving himself a rudimentary diagnosis, Johnny thought again about his troublesome fits of carefree immaturity, trying to examine them… He wondered if they were symptomatic of his mind's need to take routine vacations from the many things troubling his mind, which had increased since his long-term stay at the psych ward. He kept in mind that his mode of silliness was sometimes just a conscious ruse to keep Dr. Saunders from probing the rational side of Johnny's mind, usually when Johnny's other mental defences were too tired for a psychological fencing session. Maybe Johnny had gotten so used to adopting the kooky persona—which had only seemed kooky once it had passed—that the ruse became a real side of him (or it had unleashed a real side of him that had always been there). Maybe he'd unwittingly programmed himself to unconsciously retreat into the persona, even when he hadn't intended to.

No matter what, he was almost sure he didn't have some offshoot of Multiple Personality Disorder, contrary to what Dr. Saunders had tried to tell him once. Johnny could say that he was always aware of being the same person, fully conscious of his radical shifts from one mood to the next.

So, one-on-one counselling sessions with Dr. Saunders had proven horrible; enough to make Johnny actually miss even the most absurd group activities he'd been put through. At least whenever he was with other patients, Johnny didn't have to spend time alone with the creep.

# Chapter 4

JOHNNY TRIED TO TAKE a breather from thinking about his private sessions with Dr. Saunders, since he would only burn himself out if he didn't. As it was, the upsetting memories had made his face grow hot and his heartbeat quicken.

On rare occasions, other psychiatrists had filled in for Dr. Saunders, offering Johnny an experience that was at least non-threatening by comparison. Thankfully, they had restricted their role to counselling, rather than bringing intense psychotherapy or any talk of medication into the session. Although they were full-fledged psychiatrists, as opposed to counsellors or psychologists, they'd probably held back from doing a lot of the things they were qualified to do, likely afraid of playing with the possessive Dr. Saunders's favourite toy. Still, while those counselling sessions hadn't made Johnny feel menaced in any way, they hadn't proven especially useful, either.

One time, Johnny had tried to impart his distress to one of those replacements; some guy whom Johnny only remembered as Dr. Somebody. As remote as Johnny's hope of success had been, he'd still wanted to file an informal complaint about Dr. Saunders, as well as voice a few grievances about the state of things in general.

Johnny hadn't been sure about how well his attempt to change the nature of the conversation would be received: The session was about addressing Johnny's issues, after all, and not about validating what he had to say. He'd doubted that even the friendliest professionals around here would just let him shift focus away from scrutinizing his own faults or "ills" to talk instead about those of the world around him... especially when Dr. Saunders was going to be the hot topic of criticism.

He'd also imagined that Dr. Saunders would be a touchy subject with these people. At the time, he'd resolved to stay vigilant and keep in mind that, no matter how sincerely friendly and unassuming this new therapist seemed, Dr. Somebody was still a colleague and maybe even a personal friend of Dr. Saunders. Until Johnny was convinced that he could trust this man, he'd decided that the three best things for him to do were choose his words carefully, share only a couple of his thoughts at a time, and keep an eye on the responses of his new psychiatrist-playing-counsellor.

"So, what's on your mind?" Dr. Somebody had asked warmly, opening the session with a kindly and supportive air.

"Do you mind if I express something in hypothetical terms?" Johnny had asked, unsure of where and how to begin.

"Sounds interesting," Doctor Somebody had answered. "Why don't you give it a try?"

"Okay, pretend you're a mathematician and, because you know I'm crazy..."

"I don't think you're crazy," his substitute-shrink had interjected gently.

"Yeah, right," Johnny had replied, trying to keep any hint of cynicism out of his voice to humour Dr. Somebody. His tone had come off as a bit dismissive, quite abrupt, and eerily chipper; a combination that had made those two words sound as phoney and forced as they'd actually been.

"Anyway," he'd resumed, trying not to look self-conscious about his verbal slip-up, "Because you know I'm a bit 'confused' about things, suppose you then decide to take advantage of that:

"You tell me that two plus one equals ten or something absurd..."

Johnny had then interrupted himself to ask a quick question:

"Oh, by the way... Just to make sure that I haven't completely lost it and that we're on the same page here: Two plus one does equal three, right?"

"Last time I checked," Dr. Somebody had replied, giving Johnny a reassuring smile of good humour. "Go on."

"Okay, good. Well, anyway, I pull out three beans, put two in one palm, count them, add the other one, and then count the sum total of three. I keep counting those three beans while you keep telling me that there should be ten…

"You even tell me about some new school of mathematics I've never heard of, and that the people running it claim that all basic equations had recently been disproved for some convoluted reason or another. You also tell me that, according to the authority of that new school of thought, what I'm still seeing plainly in my own hand is no longer valid."

"Interesting."

Johnny had paused briefly, taking in how condescending the response had sounded. After a couple of seconds of uncertainty, he'd continued:

"See, in that example, you have the expertise, the textbook smarts, and the backing of this questionable school of thought, which I'm automatically supposed to believe is credible…

"Meanwhile, I have a substantial argument… in the physical form of three beans, no less. According to some, it wouldn't do me any good, though; some might just say that I shouldn't challenge your expertise, lest I embarrass myself in showing the world what a crazy backwoods plebeian I am."

"So, if I understand clearly, you think people are out to deceive or take advantage of you in some way?" Dr. Somebody had asked with calm uncertainty, giving a slight raise of his eyebrow that conveyed both intrigue and concern.

"Let's not change the subject, but… sometimes, yeah. All kinds of people out there, in all kinds of fields, will eagerly pooh-pooh at a layman who notices problems with what's being said:

"'Oh, you're just an uneducated nobody, an amateur,' is the gist of their attitude, 'You need to have my credentials in order to challenge what

I purport, no matter how plainly flawed it is, or how much you think I have ulterior motives, or how much fact-checking you do, or how fraudulent you think my school of thought is. You have to be one of us, and thus agree with our quackery, for you to be in a position to debate or criticize our thinking… which, because you're one of us, we know would never happen.'

"Does that sound fair or sensible to you?"

The therapist had only acknowledged hearing Johnny with an ambiguous humming sound, while appearing engrossed in whatever he'd been writing on his notepad.

Johnny had pressed on, probably talking a little faster than the man could write:

"Let's take this a step further: Let's say you now want to act as though your doctorate in mathematics gives you a doctorate in everything else. While it's possible for you to have knowledge or experience in other fields, we'll say that, in this hypothetical case, you certainly don't… or that you're lying through your teeth as you knowingly make a false claim, which you still insist I should believe because of your position:

"You want to tell me that the Earth is filled with ice cream, or that I'm a dog in the body of a man. You're not a geologist or a biologist, but, according to you, a doctorate in mathematics is still better than no doctorate, right? So then I'm told I should listen to you anyway, even if you don't really have a solid point… and you also lack the proper qualifications to pretend convincingly that what you say is automatically credible."

Dr. Somebody had seemed a little amused at that, though he'd remained silent, letting Johnny proceed.

"'Doesn't matter,' you might tell me, since I'm expected to take your statement at face value on irrelevant credentials… which would then actually put you in the same boat as a person without any credentials to hide behind. You're officially better educated than I am, though; and, to some, that means that your word automatically trumps mine."

"So you don't think credentials are valid?" Dr. Somebody had asked, in a tone that was more curious than accusing or incredulous.

"Don't get me wrong; I'm not talking about experts who can prove a point objectively. If the expert can actually build an argument and bring something concrete to the discussion, then I suppose all's well. After all, this hypothetical person should be able to do such a thing, if his field and expertise in it are valid.

"See, once I would have thought of an expert as someone who has the training and ability to build and present a solid case quickly and honestly. As it turns out, there are people out there who think their claims of expertise cancel out any need to explain their point, or show evidence to prove it. Those people resort to the tired, crappy argument of, 'I'm right because my school says so.' They don't think a regular person can do research of their own and raise valid counterpoints, in order to call out potential con artists.

"Then there's the issue of an expert making a point that only holds true within the framework of his field of expertise, when the field in question relies on ideas that are philosophical and unproven; you know, a school of thought that is abstract and highly-theoretical, ever-changing, and quite... debatable."

"Care to share a specific example?" Dr. Somebody had asked with only a vague hint of curiosity.

Johnny hadn't been quite ready to spell out the exact example he'd had in mind, so he'd settled on another hypothetical substitute:

"Okay... Let's say you're a certified expert in some new school of alternative medicine. Maybe you even use your separate doctorate in mathematics to bring the illusion of credibility to this questionable field. Or, maybe you suggest that your thorough understanding of this new school of alternative medicine automatically makes that school legitimate. Whether or not you tell me that your qualifications in that school stand on their own, you then act like anything you say about a person's health or wellbeing is something that everyone outside of this field should respect and agree with."

"What would I, or this hypothetical expert, claim?" Dr. Somebody had asked.

Johnny had fought off the urge to accuse Dr. Somebody of nitpicking to stifle the point he'd been trying to make. Drawing in a deep breath, he'd given the best impromptu answer he'd been able to think of:

"I don't know, maybe you're making the abstract claim that a person's offset 'energies' correlate with the severity of a physical ailment or something. It's the kind of statement that would only be meaningful to someone who believes or shares a doctorate in this same unproven field of alternative medicine.

"See, now I'm talking about a field in which abstraction and unsettled claims form its entire basis. So what if you have a doctorate in that field? As I was saying, even your doctorate in mathematics wouldn't validate this other field that you're also an expert in, since mathematics and alternative medicine have nothing to do with each other. As I've already said, your mathematics doctorate wouldn't even prove that you have expertise in another field to begin with, whether it's a credible field or not… but that's getting off-topic.

"The point is, your expertise in a school of thought isn't going to be worth much to an outsider if that outsider doesn't believe in the philosophy. After all, maybe some of the scepticism comes from the false or mistaken claims that have already come out of the field; unsettled claims that are always subject to change, and yet are always to be taken at face value when they're made.

"Say the experts in your field assert that running around in circles for twenty minutes a day is good for people, but less than a year ago, they were saying that it was the worst thing people could do to their energies, and thus their health. Nothing conclusive inside or outside the field has been proven, but its latest theory is still supposed to be immediately accepted as factual, no matter how fickle-minded that field's experts have already proven to be.

"It just doesn't make sense for you, as an expert in this questionable field of alternative medicine, to insist that people should embrace whatever you say and agree to start using a new kind of treatment on the sole basis of your expertise in this controversial field.

"Do you follow?"

Dr. Somebody had tightened his mouth in a pseudo-smile; Johnny hadn't been able to tell whether or not the doctor had any trouble understanding Johnny's discourse, which admittedly had been on the brink of rambling.

"I mean, unless I believed in the expert's field and the worldview its based on, or wanted an accredited representative of that school so I could debate its validity with him, what value would that expert's credentials have to me? If I think your school of thought is faulty, then how would your standing in it carry any universal weight, and lend any credence to the effectiveness of a new treatment that you want to foist upon me?"

Dr. Somebody had sat patiently, as if waiting for Johnny to say more. Instead of letting the silence continue and grow awkward, Johnny had carried on:

"At the end of the day, wouldn't I be convinced only after I know that this new treatment makes sense, actually works, and does no harm to the patient? Even when those criteria are met, I'd probably be supporting this expert's specific claim because he's demonstrated its value and merit, and not because he was formally educated in his controversial field. In fact, I might agree with the guy in spite of his background, if I still have reason to think his background is largely a sham.

"Even if this new field of alternative medicine does garner credibility, isn't it ultimately because its experts have made compelling and sensible arguments, that they've shown the world that their approach is effective? In other words, they can demonstrate their solutions to—or appraisals of—problems to be consistent and effective, without first requiring people to blindly accept their whole philosophy before determining its integrity."

Another long silence ensued before Dr. Somebody had eventually broken it:

"You have a lot to say." His remark had shown no sign of condescension or disdain, but it hadn't revealed any agreement or disagreement with Johnny's thinking, either. "I must say you're also very articulate."

That last bit had sounded a little patronizing.

Johnny had decided to express one more chain of thoughts before making up his mind about Dr. Somebody's trustworthiness:

"Don't even get me started on people with honorary doctorates, or these pontificating actors and other celebrities who love to tell people how to live their lives, what politics they should have, and blah, blah, blah, blah, blah.

"From the way they act, you'd think some of these people believe that their prancing around in front of a camera and being famous amounts to having a doctorate; that any point they make is automatically valid or important. 'Look at me, I'm some twit whose career is built solely on appearances, and that's what gives my words substance!'

"Regardless of how unreasonable or stupid their statements may or may not be, they behave as though their fame alone lends credibility to what they say. I wonder if any of them actually consciously exploit the dullards who like their movies or albums; you know, rally fans to support their way of thinking, even if it's something as stupid as endorsing a dictatorship.

"Even if they were to say something outright true or credible, their fame and image are still being used to validate their opinions. I mean, do these people even care if a given opinion is credible on its own merit? Some really seem to like the idea that their statements are sound—or at least regarded as sound—because of their standing as entertainers, and nothing else.

"So, they too could knowingly lie through their teeth, whoring themselves out to con artists who want to sell faulty ideas or products, using their social status as a substitute for even a pretence of expertise. At that point, you can't even say that they're exploiting irrelevant credentials from the most controversial schools of thought.

"Meanwhile, anyone daft enough to listen to charlatans in the celebrity circle is giving authority to those who have neither a valid statement nor a relevant claim of expertise.

"By the way, I'm not talking about people who get asked before speaking their mind, say during an interview. Maybe a few of them just want to assert their separateness from all the proactive loudmouths in their community of entertainers, who behave as though they speak for everyone in it.

"And, yeah, maybe some hypothetical examples don't always fit every seemingly similar situation, but I'm pretty sure mine cover all the key features that would define a lot of real-world parallels. Personally, I think my examples make for some pretty darn good models… I mean, if, say, you're an honest expert who makes solid arguments to prove a point, then none of my examples would apply to you, you understand…

"Well, what do you think?"

Dr. Somebody had only glanced up from his notepad to flash Johnny a quick smile, again acknowledging that he'd heard his patient… though it was unlikely that he'd really been listening. If he'd known what else to draw from all of Johnny's talk—specifically the especially bothersome issue Johnny had been inching towards—Dr. Somebody had shown no sign of it.

For that reason, he hadn't dared to ask Dr. Somebody if he thought Dr. Saunders's ever-changing diagnosis was a sound practice. After the session, Johnny had remained as in the dark as he'd been before it had started, still wondering if he was legitimately unwell or a drugged-up prisoner.

If anything, the session had done Johnny more harm than good, though the harm had been largely self-inflicted. Lying in bed in his quarters, Johnny had spent what must have been hours wrestling with daunting thoughts, stemming from the talk he'd initiated with Dr. Somebody. Within minutes, his thoughts had broken up and multiplied into a sea of musings, which had threatened to drown his psyche.

Now he was going through that mentally strenuous process again, this time while lying on a tabletop, in a room that looked like a place he'd worked at years ago.

A myriad of complicated ideas tore its way into his head, creating a new tier of things to think about. Unfortunately, those things came to him all at once, congesting his mind and muddying the views he'd been able to express somewhat clearly to Dr. Somebody:

He thought about people fabricating evidence to support their assertions, and ridiculing those who didn't accept it. Some guy could claim that he'd been to another planet and present a painted rock as evidence of his visit, or find a strange-coloured rock and hastily conclude that it had dropped out of the sky.

The rock wasn't evidence of anything at that point; that guy was just saying something unproven about the rock, in order to fit its existence into the scheme of either of those claims.

In the unlikely case where the guy actually had been to another planet in an unheard of galaxy, maybe he would try to give his claim a boost with false evidence, which would hurt his credibility all the same. Maybe he'd paint an ordinary rock an exotic colour, and say that he'd brought it back with him as a memento.

Inversely, some people suffered from wilful blindness when a case was brought before them. No matter what facts, sound reasoning, or even plausible ideas they were presented with, they'd deliberately ignore them. Some would refuse to acknowledge even the most humbly-expressed possibilities they simply didn't like, regardless of how plausible or implausible they were.

Maybe that guy with the rock was making a truthful statement, one that was far less difficult to prove: Maybe he was trying to tell people that what he possessed was made of a rare and precious metal. In that situation, the stubborn sceptics might refuse to even glimpse at the rock; perhaps lying and claiming that they'd already given it a look, they might not even wait for him to get the thing tested, and bring back the results. Maybe because they didn't want to believe that this guy could come across such a rare find, they might even go so far as to deny the fact that he was holding a rock of any kind.

Perhaps, thought Johnny, the example of a guy with a funny-looking rock (which he'd pulled out of nowhere) was a bit absurd and exaggerated, but it really did capture the essence he saw in those kinds of dysfunctional debates.

There were people out there who loved playing the game of technicalities to sustain their position:

"If it's not immediately in front of me, or you can't give me proof positive right this second, or you can't convince me immediately, then I refuse to consider even the possibility of its existence, even if you're only meekly suggesting it as a remote possibility. And if you do show me any evidence or try to explain yourself, then I'll close my eyes and plug my ears, so there!"

He could vividly recall feeling frustrated and dizzy after having dealt with people like that, well before he'd met Dr. Saunders. After he'd buried his once-clear recollections of specific situations, what remained were just memories of mental processes; the overall sense of having been caught up in that kind of maddening dynamic… possibly many times.

Some people resorted to rather dishonest and sneaky ways of discrediting their opposition. If they lacked the intention or capability of examining and addressing an opponent's argument directly, they would likely try to make that opponent look incapable of making a valid argument. Needless to say, resorting to smears and personal attacks was one cheap way of fending off an argument. Another one entailed the practice of revising opponents' arguments, either putting words in their mouths or omitting key aspects of what they'd said. Johnny wondered how many people consciously asked loaded questions, or knowingly made selective interpretations of (or assumptions about) what someone had said to them.

Some people would shape their perception of a person to fit whatever best indulged their overall views. They liked to presumptuously assert that you were in perfect agreement with them, or at least demonstrated the thinking they wanted you to have.

If, for instance, you had said that you would think about an idea, or were open-minded about a given subject, then they might insist that you were onboard with their views. The rather arrogant implication from this was that you were only open-minded if you were in agreement with them. If they couldn't force their understanding of you to fit their perceptual mould of how they wanted to see you—as being happily in agreement with whatever they had in mind—then they might vilify you as an unreasonable, stupid, or horrible person. In either case, those people were trying to reinvent your identity, adjusting its portrayal in their eyes (or rhetoric) to suit how they wanted to see the world and everything in it.

Then there were those cheap tricks the really obnoxious people resorted to, like character assassination. If they weren't outright lying about what a person had said or done, whether or not it related to the argument at hand, then they'd try to misrepresent the opposition's position to a broad audience. Sometimes they would attack an opponent's reputation with loaded terms that were unimaginative and insubstantial:

If you challenged or questioned a scientist's ethics or honesty, the morality of certain agendas and experiments, then proponents of these pursuits just might say that you were "anti-science." If you didn't hear out every obnoxious sales pitch, whether it was a product or an idea, then that salesman (figuratively or literally) just might accuse you of being "closed-minded." Even then, you'd only be given the arrogant benediction of being "open-minded" if you not only sat through, say, his entire timeshare seminar, but also signed on the dotted line in agreement to whatever unfair terms he had in mind.

It was just like Dr. Saunders's calling Johnny childish, paranoid, stubborn, and, yes, crazy (or "unwell") for questioning the doctor's intentions and methods. Whether or not he believed Johnny sane, Dr. Saunders would still treat him like an ignorant twit for any show of dissent. Even now, Johnny could virtually hear Dr. Saunders's voice lazily dismissing his thinking as "anti-science," "anti-progress," "anti-psychiatry," or perhaps even "anti-mental health."

("Yeah," Johnny mentally retorted, "I'm sure electroshock and front lobotomies were considered quite scientific and progressive back in their day, too.")

That brought an indignant thought to mind: What was next? Dignifying a person's right to hassle you by debating the issue? Having to explain to a person why you shouldn't be attacked on the street and mugged?

Since you weren't dealing with reasonable people to begin with, he doubted they'd listen to any well-founded objection to their invasiveness. In any case, why pander to the arrogance of any self-proclaimed authority by humouring a debate with them, in order to justify your being left in peace?

Then there were implicit personal attacks, which were sometimes combined with citing those irrelevant credentials; people might challenge their opponents' professional standing while boasting about their own at the same time:

"I'm a professional writer; what do you do for a living?" such a person might say to his opposition, when the topic of controversy had nothing to do with writing, regardless of whatever the writer's opponent did for a living. Writing had nothing to do with a discussion about, say, the moral implications of something; it didn't matter what that something was, since the job alone had nothing to do with being a moral authority.

Even if this party were to make a bold statement about whether or not standing on your head was good for your health, then he'd have to rely on a little more than a laughably pretentious declaration like that.

Johnny wondered if he really had gone crazy or was missing something; how was making an opponent merely "look bad" something to be proud of? It wasn't honest, and it certainly didn't lend any credence to the argument being made. Yet, even so, Johnny couldn't shake strong mental images of the kinds of people who indeed revelled in being crafty over being truthful, while their body language practically bragged about it.

It seemed to Johnny that a lot of people like that (or just a few loudmouthed ones) had this strange idea that their position was valid by default, and would remain that way until they could no longer falsely discredit those who dissented from their position. So, preferably in front of a third-party audience, they did what they could to make their opponents "look bad."

Some genuinely seemed to believe that the goal of appearing to be correct (to get their way) was more important than the truth or presenting their side honestly, and that made for a twisted kind of adversarial system… If those who subscribed to it didn't think it was unethical or wrong to be so conniving and manipulative, how could anyone argue or reason with them? You couldn't really expect them to care when you pointed out their lack of consistency or ethics, since they didn't value such things.

Some people seemed to think that good debaters were always right, or that winning the debate automatically made the winner's position correct. For them, the ability to push ideas with pretentious twaddle was more important than the legitimacy of the position, which the twaddle served to refute or defend.

Johnny imagined a crafty wizard of rhetoric asserting that eating dog faeces was part of a balanced breakfast, leaving the opposing debater too shocked and appalled to offer any rebuttal whatsoever. Was the silent and disgusted opponent wrong because he'd failed to put on a convincing and engaging show?

Sure, honest and thorough arguments could convey the truth about an issue, but the audience needed to be willing to listen with honesty, rather than stubbornly find excuses to discredit what they simply didn't want to hear.

One might notice the overzealous fans of a particular debater, commenting on how dangerous it was for these fans to deny the possibility that their hero could lose an argument. (Losing an argument and being on the wrong side of an issue, meanwhile, weren't always the same thing.) All the while, that critical observer could very well be speaking out of bias, either favouring the opposing position, or maybe the particular debater representing it.

That long train of thought brought another stressful consideration to mind:

He'd already talked to Dr. Somebody about how wonderful it was for one to make an argument or claim based on real-world evidence or sound reasoning, instead of relying on a school of thought that wasn't universally accepted. Well, that was all well and good when dealing with things like checking facts, or testing the accuracy, effectiveness, or consistency of a claim (while also preferably dealing with an honest person making that claim).

However, there were those debates about philosophical things, the likelihood or unlikelihood of something currently unknowable; something that relied on an intangible component, like determining the right course of action during a crisis.

For a point to have universal merit in the eyes of two or more parties—each having a different worldview—there still had to be some common ground between them; their morals and values came to mind.

It was no use trying to present an ethical solution to a problem if those you were talking to had a worldview that dismissed conventional ethics or moral "constraints."

If they didn't value or acknowledge concepts like compassion for the sick, they might not regard a pandemic as much of a problem, let alone see any need to solve it. The question of which proposed treatment was the better one got flushed right down the toilet when the people you were talking to were against helping the patients at all. Instead, they might focus on eradicating weakness in society by letting the sick die off, deeming any moral considerations outmoded and impractical.

Johnny imagined an extreme manifestation of a self-proclaimed amoral mindset: People who didn't believe in wrong (or who really liked to mess with your head) could technically shrug in the face of being called hypocrites, even after showing that they did care about their own wellbeing and protection (while still wanting to remove "undesirables" from society).

He couldn't see any way around it: Those kinds of differences between people were irreconcilable, and positions dealing with intangible issues required more than just something concrete to validate them... if any philosophical position mattered at all. Being consistent was important, he asserted to himself (while unsure of why he felt as though he were arguing with someone else).

What could you say, though, to a person who outright rejected the need for consistency… except maybe that this person was the one who probably belonged in a nuthouse?

Maybe a lot of people like that didn't really believe what they said. Either way, resorting to technicalities and cheap intellectual parlour tricks were likely to flow from unscrupulous people, whether or not they outright prided themselves on dispensing with matters of conscience. Maybe some of them just made like they were "amoral" to save face at the last minute, when they couldn't otherwise morally justify their position…

Maybe using the word "amorality" made them feel cool.

Johnny thought more about the technicalities that people resorted to when peddling their ideas, which in his mind were just tools of psychological warfare. One pseudo-philosophy in particular was now bugging him:

"Oh, nothing is the case until you convince me otherwise," some might say, even when the reality of a situation was undetermined. If there was room for multiple possibilities, ruling things out prematurely didn't make a lick of sense… especially since what might or might not have been the case could still have consequences either way. The problem was, whenever people resorted to that approach, they seemed to evade the consideration of how probable or improbable a possibility was.

From what he could tell, it sounded like they were eager to give an existing but undetermined possibility a closed-minded (and selective) dismissal. This implied that every example of an undetermined possibility was just as improbable as receiving a visit from Martians, simply because the possibility in question was undetermined. (In Johnny's mind, it was a rather derisive and demeaning way of dismissing someone.)

He'd like to see how eagerly this (usually) smugly-voiced philosophy would be applied practically, if a hungry group of these people were out in the middle of the wilderness, crowded around a strange-looking berry bush:

"Gee, guys; why don't we just go ahead and eat the berries? You know, since nobody has proven to us that they're poisonous or anything, they obviously aren't."

He somehow doubted that they'd be so confident in their school of thought then; this whole notion of, "If I don't know about it, then it doesn't exist."

Another scenario popped into his already-weary head:

One person might try to dismiss an undetermined possibility on the basis that such a thing—an occurrence or sighting—was allegedly unprecedented. Relying on that statement alone had its limits; while impossible things were, yes, unprecedented, not all unprecedented things were impossible.

In a time before aeronautics, a person could have used that line of reasoning to deny the possibility of flying machines. With that example in mind, the silliness of relying on the framework, "It hasn't happened before, so its existence is impossible," was pretty obvious (at least from what he could tell).

Simple enough.

Inversely, flying polka-dotted elephants weren't likely real, either; and that same line of reasoning might also end up being applied to deny the existence of such creatures. He doubted people would be as inclined to criticize the use of the statement in that context.

Of course, there was also a slight difference between: "It hasn't happened, so it's impossible," and, "It doesn't happen because it's impossible." However, the "because it's impossible" route would require some additional explanation; considerations of plausibility, probability, or anything else that would build a case supporting why such-and-such couldn't happen or would never be seen.

The problem was, the line of reasoning was given different degrees of scrutiny depending on the subject. Again, he really, really doubted that someone would wag a finger at someone who said:

"No one has ever seen a flying polka-dotted elephant; such a thing is impossible."

The additional qualifiers of the statement were unspoken (if even consciously thought about); he doubted most listeners would even bother to assume they were there before accepting the statement on an as-is basis.

For that reason, a person might try using the specific example of flying polka-dotted elephants as a universal model of the statement, "Its being unprecedented is equal to its being impossible."

That sneaky person might then try to liken the idea of discovering a previously unknown species of animal to the idea of witnessing flying polka-dotted elephants, derisively suggesting that the possible existence of a new animal species was fundamentally absurd. Switching concepts—from a flying polka-dotted elephant to an undiscovered species—could affect how the line of reasoning was regarded, even if it was still limited in any case.

If people wanted to enhance their ridicule of a concept, and shame those who'd purported it, they could bring up flying polka-dotted elephants. If they wanted to support and defend an idea, however, they could just as easily use the example of once-unprecedented flying machines, only using quality comparisons when they were convenient.

Such people might also falsely accuse you of relying on the argument of, "It's unprecedented so it's impossible." Maybe you had only said, "It's never happened before because it's impossible," while qualifying that statement with additional information to elaborate on why you believed such-and-such was impossible. At that point, the accusers were putting words in your mouth, tweaking what you said to suit their refutation.

Johnny himself had to be very, very careful when trying to grasp the essence of any seemingly transferable concept, lest he make wrongful comparisons between seemingly similar things.

In the end, quite a few of those discourse-related complexities came down to deceptiveness, he supposed; the lies and crooked head games people played with one another, and, sometimes, with themselves to believe whatever they stubbornly wanted to believe. He couldn't even begin to process all the innumerable ways that even a simple exchange of ideas could sour in this way. Instead, countless examples of them remained locked in his reveries as overlapping, rudimentary mental visualizations.

Right now, examples of toxic discourses were coming to Johnny's mind in the form of the unwinnable arguments he'd already had with Dr. Saunders, as well as the hypothetical ones he'd grimly anticipated having. Unless he'd stopped thinking about them, the hypothetical sort of argument would unfold in his mind, wherein Johnny was pitted against an imaginary version of Dr. Saunders. (Considering how badly the real-life arguments had gone, Johnny didn't really know why his mind was compelled to add to them.)

Imagining and remembering arguments wasn't really like literally hearing voices in his head, but it was pretty darn close. Johnny would routinely mentally challenge the legitimacy of Dr. Saunders's exercises, the inconsistency in everything he said, or his lack of professionalism and ethics (not to mention legality) when he did nasty things, like send Johnny to the Hole.

Estimating Dr. Saunders at his worst, the mentally-recreated version of the man always ended up responding to Johnny's complaints and challenges with dismissals, shrugs, or by asking "Why?" over and over again like a stubborn, petulant child who refused to listen to anything he didn't want to hear.

He forced himself to stop thinking directly about Dr. Saunders, or anyone else like him, and turned his thoughts again to the big picture:

Even if those representing one side of a debate or conflict were brimming with dishonesty about their position, or had wilful prejudices towards their opposition, those representing the other side could still be guilty of the same things. Johnny supposed it was hardly a profound or novel thought, but it gained weight in his mind when mulling it over alongside the many abstract, semi-specific shapes of toxic mind games masquerading as discussions.

If one of two opposing positions was correct, but its supporters were still dishonest about presenting it (perhaps taking a fraudulent approach), then whatever merits that correct position had only existed in spite of its representatives. Their rightness, or being closer to the truth than their opponents, was just a coincidence by that point. If they'd been consciously deceptive in making their claims, the rightness of their claim could also be unbeknownst to them.

How could they or anyone fault a person for distrusting a liar who dishonestly pushed a point, even if there was some truth to it in the end?

In his now-fevered contemplative state, Johnny had just lost track of all time, thinking about things faster than he could process them. Without the consent of one part of his mind, another obsessively tried to gather and mentally articulate everything it could, all at once; the beginnings of every example of psychological underhandedness he could imagine.

He wasn't sure how many of his examples actually tied in with the vague memories he'd consciously tried so hard to repress. Finding out would mean concentrating and unlocking his memories, which he had trained himself to refrain from doing; his aversion was now instinctive.

While second-guessing the fairness of his models—examples of crappy people to talk to, basically—he simultaneously tried slowing down his multiple trains of thought, just so he could properly see and assess one idea. The torrent of thought refused to be eased, and processing (let alone examining) any of them was getting to be too much for him to handle.

Embracing his inexplicable need—this indescribable itch of his—to expand upon what he could begin to visualize fully, he found his mind summoning far more than it could digest. (Sometimes, he was amazed that those violent episodes in his mind didn't give him physical headaches more often than they did.) He hated it when this happened; this turbulent form of introspection certainly wasn't bringing him any peace.

While his head felt ready to explode (hopefully figuratively), the rest of him felt as though it were stuck at the bottom of an ocean, struggling to swim up to the surface in vain; or, trying not to suffocate under a heap of junk, which someone had just dumped on him. The mental overload felt like something physical, slippery but heavy. It also felt alive, and out to keep him in a state of confusion. For that reason, he needed to stop and push back the onset of an emotional tsunami. He wanted mental clarity, but not at the price of burning himself out by filling his head with more than he could handle.

These feelings were also familiar. While their familiarity strongly hinted at the reason he'd been admitted here, a small recessive part of him knew that this wasn't the case.

Johnny could recall enough off the top of his head to reaffirm to himself that he'd been an ordinary person once, and—if what he was willing to remember held true—that he'd come here voluntarily, regardless of Dr. Saunders's ever-changing narrative.

He also knew that this hospital hadn't always been so... weird, even though he couldn't pinpoint the exact time things had changed so radically. Sure, things were always a little bizarre at this place, but initially they weren't quite as extreme as they were now. Over the course of what seemed like years, this place had transformed into what he could only half-jokingly describe as an externalization of how he'd felt about the world... long before finding himself under Dr. Saunders's sinister brand of care.

As if to signify the end of his violent meditations, Johnny saw three figures standing in the doorway out of the corner of his eye. He could almost physically feel the eyes of Dr. Saunders and two of his burly assistants probing him, which was enough to make his skin crawl.

# Chapter 5

JOHNNY HAD NO IDEA how long Dr. Saunders and his two goons had been lingering just outside the open door, since none of them had made a sound in all that time, however long it was. The three of them hadn't needed to say anything for Johnny to know that he was to remain perfectly still and quiet.

If he didn't, then it would be back to the Hole for him.

Johnny didn't even breathe until their shapes finally disappeared from the doorway. Once they were gone, he began to inhale slowly and quietly as he listened to the sound of fading footsteps.

Satisfied that they were gone, Johnny gasped a couple of times before resuming his normal breathing.

It was a redundant thought, but it came to him again anyway:

This place was getting to be too much.

"I don't care anymore," he whispered to himself, hoping no one would hear him thinking out loud. "I don't care if I learn that the world is about to explode, or if an alien invasion takes place right in front of my eyes...

"I'm leaving, and I'm leaving right this minute!" he hissed aloud in spite of himself.

He quickly covered his mouth with both hands in alarm; keeping it covered, he frantically looked around the room to make sure that no one was awake, or suddenly standing in the doorway.

Thankfully, his big mouth hadn't gotten him into trouble, yet.

Johnny scolded himself, straining to keep his thoughts unvoiced: Trouble would definitely come if he kept up this reckless crap, so he'd better keep an eye on himself as much as anything in his environment.

Now, if he could refrain from doing something stupid, this first part would be easy, hallucinations or no hallucinations…

After sliding his rump off the tabletop, Johnny tiptoed his way across the floor, trying to ignore the fact that it was covered with a carpet instead of white tiles. There were still no guards standing by the exit. Hopefully, the security detail would be as negligent tonight as they ever were; if all went well, they'd be frequently wandering far from their posts or skipping every other patrol now that Dr. Saunders had left for the night (or very early morning).

Reaching the threshold of the open twin doors, he peered outside with a slight wince, half-expecting to see some scowling security dude standing there with his arms folded.

There was no sign of anyone anywhere, so Johnny stepped out into the wide hallway. Turning around, he took in the sight of the sea of tables with people lying atop them. There seemed to be more tables—and more bodies—now than there'd been moments ago. The room also appeared bigger, with additional paintings and other décor completing its look; now, it was a perfect replica of the bistro, or his memory of it.

Johnny had to keep himself from letting out a yelp; this was not good.

In that second, Johnny had become re-sensitized to how disturbing the sight was, though the otherworldly aspect wasn't what was haunting him, surprisingly: He couldn't quite pinpoint what it was, but there was something more significant to seeing his former workplace than he was able to grasp completely.

What bothered him also had little to do with the environment itself, delusion or not. Generally, memories of the bistro weren't terribly upsetting. In fact, it had been one of the mellowest places he'd ever spent any significant amount of time in.

No, that wasn't the problem. Rather, it was that the transformation of his surroundings reflected the contents of his memory. His plastic environment seemed to be prying into his mind and then drawing inspiration from it.

Only now Johnny was realizing (or remembering) that his memories didn't need to be upsetting for him to feel compelled to suppress them. Bad memories, good memories, so-so memories; under no circumstances could he afford to allow himself to remember any of them.

Why was that again?

A brief understanding of the reason flickered in his mind, coming and going too fast for his brain to thoroughly process (probably because it itself was tied to a memory). However, the fleeting insight had just left him with the knowledge that his memories would cause him problems here.

In fact, he could latently recall expecting to experience these hallucinations (or whatever they were) before he'd started to have them… and long before he'd become a patient here. Presently, he wasn't at all surprised to see that a place from his past had manifested in the sanatorium.

Another layer of that insight was struggling to come back to him, insisting that his intensely out-of–the-ordinary experiences weren't delusions at all. It was also emphasizing what was really wrong with what he was now seeing, which went beyond the apparent wrongness of his circumstances:

What he was witnessing meant that he'd failed to keep his mind in check, which he'd resolved to do, for some important purpose.

Now, if only he could recall what that purpose was…

To his frustration, the insight evaporated and vanished. He wasn't sure if he could really blame his failure to recall the important stuff on the influence of this place:

A latent memory was now insisting that he'd put himself through rigorous psychological exercises before arriving here, in order to suppress his memories and prepare him for this place. Perhaps his overdoing all of that mental training was the problem, assuming he really was supposed to remember certain key details at this point.

Like his memory had tried (and eventually failed) to do, Johnny left the bistro behind, keeping his mind fixed on the future, on getting out of here. While he wanted to force himself to dig through his recollections to understand what was going on, he still had a strong inhibition against it. He'd experienced this train of thought several times already, come to think of it; even this recurring realization had always ended with his forcing himself to forget what he'd only begun to rediscover about himself and this place.

Grudgingly, he complied with his mind's orders, and erased those thoughts before they could fully resurface. For a moment, he was surprised at how easy it was for him to forget something when he tried to; a second later, he honestly couldn't remember what he'd been trying to do.

Plotting his course as he went, watching out for people and security cameras, he strode his way to the usual out-of-the-way, neglected, and always-unguarded exit on the left side of the building; specifically, the left side of the building from the perspective of someone facing its front entrance. He really didn't know why he bothered being so cautious; he'd already walked out the front entrance a couple of times, usually while a security guard had been dozing away at the reception desk.

Besides, Dr. Saunders himself had already known about Johnny's escapades; as far as anyone knew, this was just going to be another of his fruitless excursions.

As he went along, he was thankful to see that everything in the hospital (en route to the exit anyway) appeared stable, looking exactly the way it was supposed to. If the only out-of-place manifestation remained in the ward (bistro, now) then maybe the episode, whether it was in Johnny's head or not, had been a short one, and was over and done with.

While he certainly hoped so, he wasn't going to let it stop him from getting out of here.

Once he was outside, Johnny pressed forward to the main grounds from the alley between the sanatorium and its neighbouring building. At the back of the alley, a wall connected the two structures, blocking off what would have been his preferred route.

Even for this time of night, the grounds were remarkably quiet; aside from the rustle of leaves in the nearby trees, he couldn't hear a thing. Usually, he could hear the distant murmur of traffic, day or night.

So far, nothing out here had transformed into something that shouldn't have been there.

Good, good…

Johnny could have done without the air being so chilly, though. Even without the breeze, which had picked up since earlier this evening, the weather was cold enough to make his skin prickle. He supposed he should have found something suitable to wear before going outdoors. His white scrubs—prison uniform, really—wouldn't do if the weather worsened; neither would his thin shoes, which were little more than slippers.

The sky was cloudless, which assured him that at least there wouldn't be even a light drizzle.

He took a few slow steps in no particular direction, and then noticed the sudden movement of something high above. Johnny stopped, looked up, and froze at the sight of it:

A blue elephant covered in large pink spots sailed across the sky without the aid of wings, and disappeared behind one of tall buildings on the far side of the grounds.

This place wasn't just out to get him; it wanted to mock him.

Covered in goose bumps (whether they were from what he'd just seen or the weather), Johnny tried not to panic. Frantically, he looked all around him, making sure that everything else was in its proper place and form…

Satisfied that nothing else had gone funny, he calmed down a little.

Now, where to go, where to go…

The big question was: Where would he go once he was off the premises? He always asked himself that very thing whenever he tried getting out of here, but no answer ever came to him.

While he would have liked to know the layout of the surrounding neighbourhood, and where the nearest busy public places were, he hadn't become desperate or crazy enough to ask someone for directions.

Come to think of it, there was no one around for him to talk to, anyway. That was a little odd, since, even in the middle of the night, he'd still usually see the odd visitor, patient, or security guard walking about.

Johnny's first instinct was to do what he normally did on his excursions; he'd wander around awhile before sitting under a tree on the nearby hill, fantasizing about completing his getaway. After deciding that it was in vain, he would plod back to his quarters, depressed.

Then a sudden idea popped into his head:

Someone somewhere had once said something along the lines of, "Insanity is doing the same thing over and over again while expecting different results each time."

While Johnny couldn't immediately recall who'd said it or how it had been phrased exactly, one thing was clear to him: According to that definition of madness, Johnny really was off his rocker, and had already proven the point countless times.

He stopped himself from proving it yet again.

Tonight, he would break the pattern of behaviour he'd already grown sick of ages ago. Whatever he did, he refused to return to the tyranny of Dr. Saunders, the threat of the Hole, or the mysterious medications that were probably terrible for him, both mentally and physically.

For all his newfound determination, Johnny was still going to have to think a moment about what unprecedented thing he was going to try this time.

As he pondered his predicament, he also had to wonder why, of all nights, he'd decided to change course now. Though he hadn't acted yet, he knew he was actually going to stick to doing something different this time; in theory, that made no sense.

Now this was really starting to bug him: True, his pattern of pseudo-escape had indeed grown tiresome and frustrating, but he didn't think his feelings were any more or less intense now than they'd been the last few times he'd gone through this futile routine. While he could still attribute his fresh direction to the inevitability of feeling confined for too long, there was another factor coming to mind...

Something he'd hidden in his consciousness was surfacing, and, as much as he felt driven to bury it, Johnny let it remain mentally visible for just a few seconds.

Before arriving at the mental hospital, he'd had quite a thorough understanding of how his mind worked. For reasons that were unsafe to examine right now, he'd had to risk losing his memory of the true reason why he was here, and the knowledge of what this place actually was.

However, he'd somehow been able to train himself to eventually act when he needed to. He'd known that his various thought patterns would come and go, weaving together to form different combinations and, to a point, different responses. The mental strands were always continuing to bounce off one another, prompting some to emerge and others to recede at different times; an ensuing combination would always be different from the next, as subtle as that variation was. He'd theorized (and fervently hoped) that, however long his confusion would keep him delayed, he'd eventually come to the right combination of thoughts, which would propel him towards doing... whatever it was he'd come here to do.

A semiconscious aspect of his mind began wordlessly shouting at him, deterring him from examining the nature of this mysterious mission any further (and just as the subject was getting interesting).

The subject of thought combinations in general brought something else to mind; something familiar and so mysteriously profound that he actually felt a physical surge in his head. For some reason, he also had the sudden impulse to press buttons on a numerical keypad; not just at random, either. He imagined pressing a specific combination of keys over and over again, as if he were entering a combination he'd memorized by touch only. The urge to act came and went so fast, he couldn't tell exactly how long the sequence of numbers was, or how many times he'd already mentally repeated it in the past few seconds. Already inhibited from examining the details of his sudden compulsion, his mind was also forbidding him from estimating the precise numbers his finger would now be poking in the presence of a physical keypad.

Johnny wasn't sure if he'd experienced this before or not, since, if he had, he was sure he would have forced himself to forget about it.

The memory of a to-do list flickered in his mind's eye; a sort of agenda or list of orders that would have come with a lengthy briefing. As confusing as it was to perceive, the list of tasks ended with the mandate of forgetting the list… at least consciously.

Shortly after beginning to remember that last order, his mind obeyed it, leaving Johnny with only a vague understanding of why he was here.

One thing he could draw from the fuzzy picture, which his consciousness was still frantically trying to suppress, was that Johnny hadn't really been in need of professional help at all. (That, or he was a bigger crackpot than even Dr. Saunders would allege.)

That wasn't to say that Johnny hadn't had his anxiety issues and people problems in the past. In fact, all the causes of his minor breakdown, the breakdown itself, as well as his subsequent meeting with the psychiatrist remained authentic in his mind. All that maladjustment-related stuff, however, had taken place at least a couple of years before Johnny had volunteered to come to the sanatorium. As long-term and upsetting as those issues had proved to be, they'd never resulted in his being institutionalized.

However, when circumstances and the people involved had gotten to be unendurable, they'd come close to driving him to a madhouse. For that reason, he'd chosen that particular situation to serve as his cover while infiltrating this place. It was the perfect background story, since the issue (which combined some of his biggest pet peeves) had truly brought him to his mental boiling point.

Whatever had made his mind into a series of locked compartments had hidden a good chunk of his life from his conscious memory. It was still doing a pretty good job of it, too; the period between his having a minor breakdown—which had been real enough—and his arrival at the hospital wouldn't come to mind as anything more than a murky jumble.

The harder Johnny tried to focus on that period, the more violently his psyche resisted. Whoever had put him in this state, with or without his consent, was now virtually yelling at him from the past, insisting that he still wasn't ready to know anything more than he did presently... which might have been too much already.

For now, the only thing his mind permitted him to understand clearly was that he wasn't supposed to leave this place until the job was done... whatever that job happened to be. In fact, he doubted he'd even be capable of leaving until then... if his still-hazy impressions and half-suppressed memories were true.

The inhibition stubbornly continued to obscure most of these ideas as they came to mind, while trying to purge all of them from his awareness. At the same time, a peculiar compulsion was gently nudging his attention towards one of the buildings sitting on the far side of the grounds, directly opposite and facing the sanatorium.

The structure looked much older than the others appeared to be. He didn't know his architecture or periods terribly well, but it gave him the impression of something academic from the 1700s; the kind of antiquated building he would see on a university campus. Mossy patches covered parts of the otherwise grey, eroded stonework of its exterior. He wasn't sure if the greenery was supposed to be there for aesthetic reasons; or, if the walls (and maybe the rest of the building) had just fallen into a state of neglect. Standing some four stories high, it was comparatively the smallest building in the circle of structures, and yet it maintained a commanding, almost grandfatherly presence among its counterparts.

Johnny didn't know why he hadn't really noticed the building before. Granted, his problems had often kept him distracted enough to pay no attention to things that were normally obvious. However, he wondered if the thing had ever actually appeared in its present state (or at all) before now.

With suspicion, Johnny looked over the face of the building. He saw no hint of light coming through any of the windows, and no one was standing atop or near the ten or so steps leading up to the entryway. An arched impression in the face of the building outlined a theatrically large pair of wooden doors, which added scale and grandiosity to their appearance.

The building seemed to be calling to him, though only figuratively (for now).

Whatever he was looking for could be found behind those doors; without allowing him to examine why, his compulsion was certainly telling him so.

Where that external call ended and his instinctive drive began was a bit blurry. He didn't care for the fact that the vibe he got from the building and his own psyche were in perfect agreement.

For all he knew, whatever was haunting the grounds was also infecting his mind, making him only feel as though entering the place was a good idea. On the flipside, his psyche's command could have been interpreted as an external influence, which was only pretending to be his psyche… he supposed.

Cautiously, he made his way up the steps before turning around to survey the grounds. The entire area was still deserted, which was almost a shame; half of him was hoping that someone would approach to hinder him before he could touch the handle of either door.

No such thing happened: After spending a minute or so dillydallying, Johnny slowly reached up to grasp the handle of the right door.

The door wasn't locked, although it was a little heavy to pull open.

Trying not to waste time thinking about whether or not this was a good idea, Johnny stepped inside.

There was no foyer on the other side of the entryway; just a straight hallway lined with closed doors on either wall. While it was lit poorly, he could see that the florescent bulbs in the ceiling were not only working, but also hard on the eyes to look at directly.

The drab, mostly grey interior didn't have the period look that the outside had, though it did still convey a sense of age and also brought to mind a college or school. The floor was clean but ugly; the thick tiles had a design of black and brown speckles over a grey background.

Though all of the unmarked, metal doors along the walls were closed, he imagined that they probably led to seminar and study rooms, as well as small lecture halls and offices. Along either wall, the doors alternated between deep blue and bright orange in colour, probably coated with spray-paint. The two lively colours didn't so much weigh against their sombre surroundings as they did clash with them.

Nonchalantly walking along as he looked around, Johnny wasn't sure if this place had anything unusual about it. The inside and outside of the building didn't match, which probably meant that something was out of whack, deviating radically from the way it normally was. For all he knew, the existence of the whole building, inside and out, could have been out of the ordinary.

The tackiness of the hallway wasn't quite enough to brand it unusual, though the area did have an unsettling quality about it that he couldn't quite describe… and the hall did stretch on a lot longer than he imagined the dimensions of the building could contain. There were no intersections or bends in the passage, which had no end in sight.

Feeling uneasy, Johnny began thinking about the Hole—specifically, the maze of hallways in it.

Why, oh why, was his compulsion telling him to continue forward without looking back?

Johnny stopped when he noticed a brown door to his right; the first door he'd come across that wasn't blue or orange. It was also the only one he'd seen so far to have a window in it, through which he could see a stairwell, with a wide flight of stairs going up.

The lights inside were flickering a little, just enough to add to the similarity it had to the stairwells in the Hole.

In spite of what he'd felt driven to do, Johnny refrained from entering, and instead resumed his linear walk ahead.

He hadn't noticed the precise moment the hall had changed, but it definitely had: Now, the walls were covered in vertical strips of rough and unfinished wood, the surface of the floor was a reflective creamy brown, and small spotlights hung from a glossy black ceiling.

Doors still lined either wall, alternating between deep blue and bright orange. Unlike before, however, there was a little plaque on each. Even before approaching the nearest one, which was adorning a blue door to his right, he could see that a name had been inscribed on the sign in gold letters.

It read: "Dr. Somebody."

Johnny might have believed that some of the sanatorium staff had offices in other buildings, but this was obviously wrong.

Johnny reaffirmed the obvious to himself:

"Dr. Somebody" was just a throwaway nickname Johnny used because he couldn't remember the guy's real name. Since Johnny had kept that name in the privacy of his mind, there was no way that Dr. Somebody could know about it… even if Johnny were to entertain the idea that Dr. Somebody and Dr. Saunders had decided to play a joke on him.

It seemed that the world, at least within the hospital, was playing another one of its sick jokes… Again, the distortion of his surroundings involved something that came from his mind.

Impulsively, Johnny checked the plaque of the door on the opposite wall, one of the orange ones:

"Dr. John Richard Saunders," it read.

Usually, seeing the name in print was enough to send him into a childish fit of obnoxiousness; the closest thing Johnny had to an external expression of anger.

Now, it was making him tense with dread.

Johnny had to get out of here, which, he supposed, meant retracing his steps and going where he "should," according to his compulsion. He still didn't want to enter the stairwell, even while that part of his psyche nagged him, more overbearingly than before. Johnny wondered which side of his mind was stronger: The fearful part, or the one that was consumed by this mysterious sense of duty.

Well, at least he did until he realized that he was already walking back towards the stairwell, in spite of himself.

Reluctantly, Johnny allowed himself to comply with whatever was ordering him through the door and up the stairs. His body practically drove itself along as each of his legs stretched up to ascend two stairs at a time. He reminded himself of an impatient child, filled with energy and eager to get somewhere; however, there was nothing regressive about his conscious state of mind (thankfully).

If he managed to hold on to his rational side, then maybe he would be able to survive whatever he was dragging himself into.

That brought a few unpleasant thoughts to mind: He thought of how desensitized he'd grown to things that would normally tear a person's mind apart, and how accepting he was of his current circumstances.

Yes, he was eager to try something, virtually anything, to break out of his pattern of failed escape attempts; but, he could be doing something self-destructive right now. Coming from the part of his mind that was hiding things from his awareness, this compulsion could have been due to madness. His compulsion, or whatever was inspiring it, could have been reckless in its aim. For all he knew, something malicious could have been controlling him from afar, or from within his mind.

As much as that elusive part of him was insisting otherwise, Johnny couldn't fully trust that it knew what it was doing, and that he was in good hands. If this thing inside him was so trustworthy, then why was it being so secretive? Every time he tried to unearth just a little more information about the true nature of his circumstances, that part of his mind virtually slapped the rest... like it was still doing now.

Having no idea how he'd ended up with a splintered consciousness was a big problem for him; what was this part of him that was concealing things while giving him orders? He was naturally inclined to think that he'd done this to himself at some point, or had at least consented to having it done to him. Still, he couldn't say for sure, which bothered him.

How did he even know for sure that this voice (which didn't actually speak) was really a sliver of his own consciousness? Maybe the Hole or some other crap Dr. Saunders had subjected him to had made Johnny's mind this way, injecting his consciousness with some foreign influence for whatever nefarious reason. It was possible that Johnny could still be the subject of some diabolical experiment, involving the implantation of voices in his head where they hadn't previously existed.

Maybe the presence couldn't have any intentions at all, benevolent or malevolent, because it was purely a delusion that was symptomatic of another issue. Perhaps it was just a side effect of something else that had been done to him; in that case, the guiding "voice" was a symptom of his damaged brain, and not a ploy that someone had intentionally devised.

If what he was listening to lacked any aspect of real consciousness— even as a set of designed, mentally-implanted instructions—then it was leading him along randomly, inevitably to a place where no part of him wanted to go.

Then there was the suddenness of its manifestation: Was he supposed to feel reassured that a presence in his head had sprung to life without warning and was now running the show?

Well, the presence certainly thought so.

Between reassuring him that it was there to help him, it was also insisting that he wasn't experiencing hallucinatory fits, and that he'd never experienced hallucinatory fits. Everything he'd seen, heard, or otherwise sensed, no matter how seemingly unrealistic and inconsistent, had been real and did have an explanation behind it, though he'd have to wait to get it.

If that separate part of his mind could speak it would have told him that, yes, the phenomenon was acting up again, but he shouldn't panic: What was happening to him, again, was coming from the world around him, and not from insanity.

It also filled him with the unarticulated understanding that, as far as astonishing things went, there would be a few whoppers to come.

Maybe it was a bit submissive for him to do so, but Johnny accepted what the presence in his head was telling him. Besides, he was also getting a little tired of constantly fretting over his mental health. Moreover, with all the external factors about the world of the hospital to be concerned with, he could no longer afford to stop and worry obsessively about the reliability of his mind.

Johnny supposed that, in the end, he really didn't have a good alternative to what he was already in the middle of doing. For now, he'd have to hope that this inner quasi-voice of his knew what it was talking about. If he ever wanted his problems resolved, he would have to play along with this shady side of his psyche for the time being.

Hopefully it wouldn't lead him to a predicament worse than death.

Johnny stopped his ascent at the first door he came to and nervously approached the stairwell door, which, to his irritation, had no window. He opened it slowly and, keeping the door propped open with one hand, stepped halfway outside. Continuing to stand quietly in the threshold, he scanned what looked like a hallway, which was significantly wider than the one downstairs.

As unusual as it looked, at least it didn't resemble anything he'd seen in the Hole.

While the floor and ceiling were coated in a shiny black material, the walls were made up of smooth green bricks—large rectangular blocks, actually—with no mortar joining them. The surfaces of the bricks glittered, as though their maker had mixed small fragments of real emerald and flecks of gold and silver into a base material, which resembled emerald-green ceramic.

The passage, which had no end in sight in either direction, was lit well enough, neither too dark nor too bright for his eyes to see everything clearly. The illumination was also as stable as it was even, all throughout the area.

Seeing no light source he could identify, Johnny wondered if the light was coming from the small gems and metallic particles imbedded in the walls. While they weren't glowing, he noticed that they did gleam and sparkle as he watched them without moving his eyes.

Of course, if he was in the middle of a delusion—or, if reality was in the middle of defying its own rules again—then he supposed his trying to explain the makeup and origin of his surroundings was pointless.

Finishing his exit from the stairwell, Johnny hesitantly turned left and began swiftly skulking his way forward, doing his best to stay quiet without slowing down. There were no doors or side passages on either wall, making the route easy enough.

In his head, Johnny began counting, deciding that if nothing about the passage changed by the time he reached one hundred, he'd defy his compulsion and go back to the stairwell. He hadn't counted to fifty before he suddenly approached the end of the hall. Since he'd been staring straight ahead as he'd walked, he should have seen the open entryway long before he did.

With a mental sigh, he reminded himself—yet again—that his attempts to make sense of what he saw (or didn't see) were a little passé at this point.

Startled, he stopped a few paces away from the wide opening. Hesitantly inching his way closer to it, he then came to another stop right at the threshold. Even before taking a good look though the entryway, he could already tell that the chamber was enormous. Like the hall, its walls were a glittery emerald green, and its floor a smooth, reflective black.

Johnny held his breath a moment, whether out of instinctive caution or out of shock from the most notable thing—or, rather, things—in the room.

# Chapter 6

JOHNNY NEEDED A MOMENT to comprehend what he was looking at. On first glance, they looked like big water tanks, which were connected to machinery and filled with something really disgusting.

The containment devices appeared identical to one another. Each was made up of an upright rectangular glass aquarium—about eight feet tall and five feet wide—sitting atop a dark grey metallic base, which added another two feet to its overall height. The round stands were covered in white and red lights, as well as transparent panels revealing wires and circuitry, which looked removable. Heavy-looking tubes protruding from each stand were plugged right into the surrounding floor; a mix of black rubbery hoses and flexible-looking metal pipes.

Johnny tried to avoid looking directly through the glass of the containers, knowing he wouldn't care for what he saw hovering in each tank, submerged in sickly-green, translucent (almost transparent) liquid. Deciding to get the inevitable over with, however, Johnny let his eyes settle on the putrid-looking fleshy masses.

While they brought to mind a collection of specimens, he was surprised that his stomach didn't heave on him.

Each case held one specimen, which remained vertically centred between the bottom of the tank and the liquid's surface. They varied a little in size, but each one was at least big enough to take up about two-thirds of its respective residence.

While each body was unique, they all had the common feature of being grotesque; he'd even say monstrous. Of the creatures he could see from where he was, none of them appeared humanoid, or identifiable as any specific animal he was familiar with. Sure, every one of the beastly things had at least a few recognizable physical traits, but their body parts were crudely mismatched, often disproportionate or malformed in some way.

He saw the kinds of body parts that belonged on primates and other mammals, reptiles, insects, and birds; or, to be precise, a mixed combination of said varieties on the same body. Because of the green fluid, the exact colour of each body part was difficult to discern, at least without staring at it for too long. As it was, the freakish anatomy of each complete body was a lot for his eye to take in.

Of the organisms he could see, each had more than two eyes; one of them had a big pair that belonged on a fish, with a single lupine-looking eye between them.

That specimen in particular also had a snout and mouth that reminded Johnny of a young hippopotamus, and a row of what looked like claws growing downward from its chin. A sizable beak neighboured the mouth, while the comparatively small wings of a bat were located where one would expect to find the specimen's ears. Dark, coarse-looking fur covered parts of the strange animal's otherwise bald, bloated body, which extended behind its face; the whole creature looked like a gigantic, grotesque head in the overall shape of a short, fat cigar.

That was just the beginning of the eclectic anatomy these things had…

Quickly looking over the others, he saw hideous combinations of scales, gills, hair, skin, and exoskeletons covering bodies with appendages of all kinds, including the tails of everything from giant rats to lizards. (He noticed a couple of them had three tails, each from a different genus.)

There were plenty of beaks, snouts, and even an elephant trunk… There was no shortage of the kinds of noses, mouths, and ears that these things had among them. He saw a few ambiguous orifices, too, two or more to a creature—but he didn't want to think about what those were supposed to be, if not malformed mouths. The creatures also tended to have excess organs, which made the list of total body part varieties skyrocket.

Johnny was quite disturbed to see a lifelike blob staring off into space with its eight eyes. Among the eyes, two asymmetrical cavities were situated atop a raised, bony surface, which suggested an underdeveloped nose. The large lips of the creature's humanoid mouth contrasted with the set of gigantic antlike mandibles protruding from its side, which were positioned to open and close vertically. While its fins and gills clearly belonged to an aquatic creature, the furry patches of its body definitely looked mammalian. Meanwhile, the scaly sections of its skin appeared reptilian, while neighbouring feathered areas seemed authentically birdlike.

No aspect of any creature in here looked artificial. Not only could he see a seamless fusion of body parts, but also an overlap of their features. It was difficult to classify a furry part as mammalian when it looked like it belonged on an insect, or a scaly part as reptilian when it otherwise resembled something vaguely humanoid.

He wasn't sure if the grotesques were conscious or even alive. He suspected the latter, since they appeared to be hooked up to a life support or monitoring system: Two black rubber tubes emerged from each body, connecting it to the base of its individual tank.

So far, he didn't see any sign of movement aside from the subtle bobbing of their bodies in the liquid…

Streams of air bubbles began flowing in the tanks, sporadically escaping from the creatures' ever-open orifices. Johnny wondered if they really had just started doing that, because he was sure he'd seen nothing of the sort since he'd entered the chamber. Perhaps they were starting up again after taking a break, he thought flippantly. He doubted that he'd simply failed to notice the activity before now, even though most of his attention had initially been drawn to the creatures themselves.

His ears could actually make out a gurgle from each tank whenever the intermittent jets of air rushed to the liquid's surface. The gentle sound of random bubbling echoed throughout the room from different directions, presumably from tanks out of his view. He noticed that the only thing covering the top of each tank was a grid of thin metal wire, which accounted for the audibility of the sound. Beneath the soft chorus of bubbling that came and went, he could also hear a low electronic hum filling the chamber; every once in a while, its pitch would bend down slightly. Whether or not the machines were collectively generating the sound, the hum contributed to the unsettling ambience the devices and their inhabitants exuded.

To his surprise, the only odours in the place were the smells of rubbing alcohol and medicinal chemicals, as the sights in here made his nose anticipate something rank and putrid.

Evenly spaced from one another, the machines were situated in a row of seven, parallel to the room's width. Looking between the two nearest tanks before him, he could see what looked like another six rows of the large containers. From where he was now standing, right in the entryway, it seemed like each tank was spaced about eight feet away from its respective neighbours on all sides. Doing a little mental math, combining the size of the tanks with the floor space between them, he estimated the chamber to be almost a hundred feet in length and width. If Johnny wanted to nitpick and treat his estimates as precise, then the room would have been ninety-nine feet by ninety-nine feet...

He had to admit that sometimes he really did choose the strangest things to distract himself with when facing astronomically disconcerting circumstances. Still, it hadn't taken him long to make those estimates...

If only his whole mind were in such good working order, he mused.

Supposing that he'd have to do it eventually, Johnny took his first couple of steps into the chamber, while keeping away from the tanks.

Once he managed to wrest his eyes away from the grisly sight of the organic oddities, he was able to notice the big rectangular screens built into the walls. The displays were unilaterally fifteen feet up from the floor, and each was about ten feet wide and eight feet high. There were three positioned evenly from one another on each wall, including the one behind him.

The monitors displayed red and yellow symbols against a black background, which flickered in and out of existence, sometimes scrolling vertically or horizontally. He wasn't sure if the characters were pictographs, letters, or numbers. Some of them were horizontally grouped together as though they were supposed to form words, though they could have been mathematical equations or some other abstract form of notation he'd never seen before.

To his perception, it was all gibberish. For all he knew, the images weren't meant to be read, instead just looked at. Perhaps they were just kinetic decorations for nonexistent spectators… well, unless intruders like Johnny and the bottled creatures counted as spectators.

Johnny was about to ask himself, both mentally and rhetorically, "Just where on Earth is this place?" The question was cut short with a cryptic answer, coming from that elusive part of his consciousness that had brought him to this place:

"You're close, and that's all you need to know," it would have said if it had an audible voice. It would have also told him to keep his mind as quiet as possible in here. In its own way, it still managed to get the message across.

Keeping close to the walls without actually touching them, trying to stay as far away from the holding tanks as humanly possible, Johnny began to make his way along the edge of the room in a clockwise direction.

Hopefully, something would come to his attention and give him an idea of what to do next.

As many times as he tried looking away from them, his eyes kept gravitating towards the suspended creatures, which had begun to jerk and twitch spontaneously. They looked like they were in a state of stressful sleep, as if bad dreams were agitating them.

They also looked ready to wake up any second, assuming they weren't conscious already.

Johnny really hoped they weren't acting up because they'd just become aware of his presence and found it bothersome.

In a perverse sort of way, the sight had become sort of entrancing.

Looking up to tear his attention away from the ugly things for just a minute, Johnny saw the ceiling for the first time; he had to admit it was a bit peculiar that he hadn't given it so much as a glance until now.

At least fifty feet up, he could see a network of suspended, unilateral platforms, which were either made of—or coated with—the same glittery green material covering the walls. He couldn't see whether or not something was connecting them to the ceiling. However, there were definitely no supports bracing them from underneath.

Through the spaces between the platforms—which probably served as walkways—he could see a ceiling as black as the floor. It was hard to tell exactly how high it was, but he was still sure that it was no less than twenty feet above the intricate, almost circuit-like maze of paths.

His eyes began tracing the various routes of the platforms until he noticed a vertical column, which extended all the way down to the floor, its base disappearing behind the specimens' homes. It looked like a giant, upright pipe made of a sleek forest-green metal. As far as he could tell, it touched the ground somewhere near the centre of the room, in the middle of the sea of containment devices.

He didn't even have to listen to that compulsion in his head to know that it would prod him towards the shaft, so he could take a good look at it. Unfortunately, getting there meant proceeding between the tanks while trying not to jump or scream every time one of their occupants made sudden a spasm.

Trying to quell his fear and prepare himself to press onward, he was about to think to himself that things weren't likely to get worse or stranger than they already were.

Then he stopped himself, as a horrible realization dawned on him:

His attempt to console himself could very well bring about something disastrous. If whatever governed the workings of reality here could hear his thoughts, then he had no doubt that it would take delight in showing him just how much worse things could get.

No matter what, though, it was a little late to turn back now.

One thing (the latest of many things, anyway) was really bugging him, though:

Johnny was sure that he'd already taken a good look in the direction of the column when he'd first arrived at the entrance to the chamber, so why hadn't he noticed it there before?

Instead of trying to figure out an answer to that, he once again resigned himself to the concept that reality in this place wasn't stable. As much as he should have been desensitized to it by now, the sudden appearance (or rearrangement) of things still hadn't ceased to startle him.

Then a voice, eerily similar to his own, sounded in Johnny's head, forming stunningly clear and audible words:

"Nothing in reality is stable," it rebutted dismissively. "The world is an absurd place. You're deluding yourself if you see anything rational in it."

Johnny would often hear, remember hearing, or imagine hearing that kind of statement from someone who was trying to confuse him, usually to defend a position that reason would deem indefensible. Statements like that would also prompt Johnny to begin one of those long exhausting mental arguments with himself.

Now was not the time for a long session of debate with an imaginary schmuck, he told himself. He wasn't sure if the intrusive voice represented a recreation of one who actually existed or it was an archetypal composite of several.

The vivid and overbearing quality of the voice was unprecedented, though. It really did sound like a separate speaker who'd somehow found a way to tap directly into his thoughts.

He wasn't sure which idea was worse: A telepathic intruder badgering him from within his mind, or, for the first time he could remember, actually hearing imaginary voices in a psychotic state.

"In fact," it continued, "The capacity to reason is an illusion. Understand that the human mind has the tendency to make whatever it perceives appear rational, while nothing ever truly is."

Now that was just irritating… Johnny's guiding compulsion was telling him to ignore the statement, but he couldn't resist responding to it with his own clearly articulated thoughts:

"Not a fan of the scientific method or the laws of physics, are we? Or are you just one of those people who like to dismiss the ability to reason arbitrarily; or, whenever it's convenient for you?

"If reason doesn't exist and perceiving it is delusional, then how is it that you are able to assert anything at all, including the point you're trying to make now? If you really believe that, then that's a bit of a paradox; how can you trust that belief, let alone confidently try to impart it to me or anyone else?

"That statement of yours isn't going to be any more rational or true than anything else anyone could say. I mean, if nothing observable or perceived can be trusted, then how can you even trust your own statement? How am I to trust any statement you make without partaking in the so-called delusion that you say is reason?"

"So people don't see patterns or meaning where it doesn't exist?" asked the voice, as if to chide him.

"I never said that!" he snapped aloud, before returning to keeping his words in his mind:

"If a person gets a math question wrong, does that mean there's no right answer? According to your logic, then math equations cease to exist because they don't really have a correct answer."

"Didn't I just say that there's no logic?" asked the voice, sounding amused.

"You're being ridiculous!"

"Exactly!"

In spite of his better judgement cautioning him against it, Johnny countered that:

"If the whole world's ridiculous, then how is absurdity observable, which needs to be the case in order to coin the term 'absurd'? If you're even using the word, then you are acknowledging an observable contrast between ordinary and randomly extraordinary things…"

Like the freaks filling this room, he unconsciously added.

That last punctuating remark had come quickly and spontaneously, though he wasn't sure why he felt inclined to worry about whether or not the voice had just heard it.

Hold on... First of all, was he now convinced that the voice was something truly separate from him? Second, what difference would his comment about the specimens make to the voice, even if it were someone else's?

Did Johnny's intuition know or strongly suspect something that his conscious mind didn't?

In any case, the voice made its counterpoint:

"What you're experiencing now is just the next level of the true universal reality," the voice insisted. "The one most people don't see."

"Next level? To bring up degrees of anything—including absurdity— is to acknowledge the existence of different degrees. Weren't you just saying, basically, that the whole world is always this weird and unstable all the time? If my ability to perceive reason were a delusion, then the idea of reason would only be in my head. Now you're saying that the illusion of reason exists in reality, fooling my perception into seeing it. Look, if everything is extraordinary, then nothing is; you wouldn't even have a 'next level' of reality to introduce."

"How many times does a person see a pattern where it doesn't exist, or try to draw meaning from something that has none?" it asked again.

"So, drawing the wrong conclusion about an observation automatically means that there is no correct conclusion to be drawn whatsoever? Tell me; is the existence of chance or randomness equal to the absence of logic in your thinking? And I suppose you're also going to tell me that the existence of chance negates the existence of order all together?"

If this voice—or anyone sharing in its assertion—was trying to suggest that the existence of chaos was equal to absurdity, of reality becoming surreal, then that suggested more than just the existence of one thing automatically disproving the existence of its opposite. That would also mean that concepts cited as one half of a pair of opposites were more or less synonyms, just because they could be filed into sets of opposites.

Slowing down his thinking, as if he were having a mental discourse with an imbecile, he made the mental note that opposites weren't necessarily interchangeable just because they were opposites. You could cite pairs of opposite concepts like "living and dead," "male and female," and "black and white," but trying to equate genders to colours or to the state of being alive or dead didn't work. Disorder and absurdity were not synonyms just because each of those concepts had an opposite; order and lack of absurdity weren't the same thing.

How on Earth was observing chance the equivalent of drowning in ridiculousness?

In addition, chaos and order could still coexist independently; something like imbalance, however, required the concept of balance. A thing could work properly without ever having been broken, but being broken came from the concept of something's capacity to work properly.

Again, keeping in mind that not all sets of opposites were comparable, the concept of "absurdity versus normality" still seemed to be a reasonable parallel to "broken versus working properly."

Johnny had heard it all before, but it never ceased to be exasperating; this voice in particular was trying to suggest that Johnny had always lived in a world where his surroundings were arbitrarily unstable in a surreal way.

Johnny had also grown sick of things people said to con anyone who'd listen. Some seemed to find sophomoric pseudo-philosophical head games funny, and would take an argumentative position to be disruptive and derail any serious discourse that didn't go their way.

The voice still didn't answer Johnny's last response to it. However, Johnny got the sense that the source of that voice found the mental fencing session entertaining; or, at least the stress Johnny was now experiencing.

His head was starting to feel clouded, and it was becoming difficult to keep focused on what he and this voice were actually talking about.

"I don't care how tangible all this stuff is; it isn't normal!" he bellowed in frustration. His thoughts, never mind articulation, were starting to become muddy.

The voice reminded him of the sorts of people who'd disingenuously deduce that, because falsehoods existed in the world, there were no absolutes, that nothing in existence was actually true. It was a lot like saying that, if something didn't have a logical explanation, then there wasn't one to discover, when perhaps it was currently out of the observer's reach or the observer's capacity to understand.

Even before coming to the sanatorium, Johnny had listened to plenty of people who would seem to revel in that idea, using it as an excuse to spew some dishonest claim or another. All the while, those same people would still expect people to take their assertions as being "true" at face value, regardless of how inconsistent that expectation was. Since some favoured the idea of existence having no consistency, Johnny supposed they might use that as an excuse to dispense with having to account for their own inconsistent stances. Such a rationale essentially boiled down to, "Nothing is true, but what we say is true… and what we say isn't consistent, because nothing is consistent."

"You can't even define normal," the voice guffawed.

Johnny couldn't believe this: The voice very well knew how Johnny was applying the word "normal"! Besides, it had already acknowledged the concept of absurdity, and one's capacity to perceive it.

The voice, or the entity using it, seemed to share in Johnny's supposedly wayward perception, since it hadn't said, "Absurdity? Surreality? I have no idea of what you're talking about."

Then Johnny heard it:

"Absurdity? Surreality? I have no idea of what you're talking about."

"Ha! Too late! That's not what you'd said earlier!"

"That's what I'd meant to say; you just misunderstood me," it replied.

"Liar!"

"All right then, just what did I say?" asked the voice, sounding genuinely confused or maybe even forgetful of the conversation they'd just had moments ago.

Johnny gave up, letting out a sigh of exasperation. If it didn't get its way, then the voice in his head was going to do everything it could to ensure that the conversation went nowhere.

From what he gathered, Johnny was to accept every inconsistent, over-the-top, and bizarre thing he'd seen as being no different from the world outside the madhouse. So, among other things, the appearance of spotted flying elephants—especially when he'd just thought about the concept a moment before—was nothing remarkable.

Johnny could now feel the voice continuing to push the idea on him, no longer even using words to force it into his mind: The phenomena he'd witnessed here were nothing phenomenal.

Numerous times, Johnny had thought about the wanton absurdity of the outside world, which he'd always seen come out of human madness and deception. At most, the concrete phenomena of his world in the hospital had come off as an outward representation of the insidious, consciously devised attempts some people made to confuse, deceive, and manipulate others, as well as themselves.

Aside from the voice now pestering him, who in their right mind would assert that an absurd scenario of surreal proportions—even a hypothetical one—was literally no different from typical existence, even at its most capricious?

He felt as though he were in a nightmare, wherein an oppressive force—out to distort his perception and keep him malleable—had taken the physical form of the hospital compound. Maybe he really was experiencing a painfully long dream, he thought; perhaps he was in an induced coma. If that were the case, then the tangible madness was only symbolic of the mundane kind of absurdity that came from really sick people.

Even now, Johnny was trying not to think of the ruthless psychopaths and raving psychotics out there who loved to peddle "no absolutes" as a foundation to get you to see the world the way they wanted you to. That, or state that they were being consistent when they weren't, so they could accuse you of being crazy whenever you noticed their deceptions.

No matter what, his world had never, ever been this messed up in the tangible sense before he'd come to the hospital.

The voice spoke again:

"Why do you even care about what's going on around you in this world of ours, anyway? Just live with it."

"Why? Because I live in it, maybe?" Johnny had no idea if he'd just voiced his words aloud.

"We all live in it," replied the voice dryly, talking down to Johnny with haughtiness.

Now, Johnny couldn't tell if the voice sounded like his own or Dr. Saunders's.

Either way, it conveyed the attitude of people who were dismissive out of antipathy; or, who had something to prove, eager to scoff at whatever you said, brimming with condescension. Sometimes, their argumentative and hasty rebuttals came out of contrarianism, to flaunt their "mighty intellect." Sometimes, they were just making a lazy dismissal of a point they didn't want to hear, because it criticized something they were protective of. Sometimes, they just wanted to be playfully annoying.

Thoughts of them reminded Johnny of the self-satisfied type who, with a preening air, picked apart a person's wording, rather than making a valid point or counterpoint. Such people would say things like:

"When people complain about society, they fail to notice that they are a part of it!"

Many times, the person being ridiculed was just talking about a prominent social attitude or practice, a popular fad, or something else that was perceived to be common. Whether or not the actual point was valid, the eager critic didn't address that issue at all. Instead of adding to or refuting the real point, he or she chose to be petty and pedantic, changing the subject to focus on the choice of words that were used, which could have possibly been better.

The eager critic could have asked for clarification about what was meant by "society," or could have made a quick side note about the speaker's wording, while still saying something relevant to the point, but no… If anything, the nitpicker seemed to want to shift attention from the point, thereby evading it.

Granted, some people did resort to extreme generalizations when they talked about "society," acting as though they had you and every other stranger all figured out while trying to exclude themselves in their commentaries. Often, they actually reminded him of the same critics who badgered other people about their wording, deliberately ignoring the meaning of those words in favour of an easy target to wag their fingers at pretentiously. (Both types were two sides of the same coin, when he thought about it.)

Maybe some of those people would grow out of it one day, Johnny thought.

Realizing that he was getting off-topic in his mental wanderings, Johnny grudgingly mustered a response to the voice's remark:

"That's not an argument," snapped Johnny in his thoughts. "Whether or not we live in the same world is irrelevant. I can only speak for myself, so I address my position and my reason for it. Your also living in the world doesn't mean you would be concerned about what's going on, and I'm pretty sure my point addresses that."

Johnny let out a sigh and, in spite of his better judgement telling him to stop, he continued:

"If you're condoning, complacent towards, or complicit in what's going on around here, then I wouldn't expect you to be concerned, just like anyone else who's out to make this place as unendurable as possible.

"I'll bet you've never even lived outside of this compound," challenged the voice, changing the subject.

"That's… that's…" began Johnny aloud, trailing off.

Was the voice being serious?

"Oh, and anecdotal evidence is not admissible," interjected the voice hastily, as if to pre-emptively shut down whatever Johnny would say to combat it. "Yes, you're personal account proves nothing," it added quickly, sounding reassured and pleased with itself.

It was a childish rendition of what Dr. Saunders would say whenever he wanted to silence a person's challenge to his claim, in a really quick and cheap way…

Dr. Saunders had often said things about Johnny's past that weren't true, which Johnny would contest. A few times, Johnny had even braved digging into his memory to recount what had or hadn't actually happened during a specific time.

True, Johnny couldn't technically prove a personal account to a listener by just talking about it. Yes, a person's testimony, without any additional evidence, wouldn't hold up in a court of law.

However, Dr. Saunders and those like him (including this voice, it seemed) took things a step further than that: If Johnny didn't offer more than his statement, they acted as though Johnny's firsthand knowledge simply didn't exist in anyone's eyes, including his own.

Time and time again, the man had simply refused to consider anything that existed outside his pigheaded views.

For instance, whenever Johnny had mentioned detesting the company of certain types of people (or had expressed reservations about talking to someone specific), then Dr. Saunders would try to "correct" his thinking, simply because he disliked Johnny's statement. Among other things, he would insist that Johnny was an introvert who was so painfully shy that he was socially inept.

Johnny remembered how members of the staff had often boasted about how highly rated the hospital was, and what a great reputation its mental health facility had. Every time he'd heard something like that, he could almost feel a fist punching him in his gut. He knew better than most that the glowing claims were untrue, yet his personal experience would mean nothing to anyone who refused to believe him.

In the end, when he'd thought about saying something to refute the hospital's acclaim, he hadn't bothered. He'd known then that his account would have been brushed aside without a second thought; officially, because it was anecdotal… and because it had come from a crazy person. No matter how certain he was of what he'd been thinking or doing on a specific occasion, if he didn't have a tangible way to share what he'd seen or experienced, then he shouldn't have believed it himself... or so said the likes of Dr. Saunders, who still expected Johnny to blindly accept even his most unsubstantiated conjecture as fact. Johnny still found such deceptive principles offensive.

As much as Johnny had given up on trying to get Dr. Saunders to listen to him, memories of those exchanges still haunted him. While his statements of indignation would repeat in his head, he would also begin to think of the shadows of other irritatingly similar exchanges, which had taken place years before he'd found himself in a sanatorium.

Those sorts of people didn't accuse him of lying, either; they insisted that they knew better than he did, and that their hypotheses had the power to overwrite whatever he knew. To Johnny, getting accused of being delusional or imagining things was almost worse than being called a liar; especially after these people had then told him to embrace their lies.

(He would never, ever submit to the idea that he was staying in the best hospital in the country, if not the world!)

In their demented eyes, your license to trust in your own memories and experiences was contingent on whether or not they found what you said convincing. If you knew something they didn't, and they refused to consider that concept, then what you knew officially didn't exist... especially when they didn't want to find what you said convincing. Yet, their speculative proclamations still supposedly trumped whatever firsthand knowledge you had. In their thinking, the burden of proof didn't go both ways.

Then there were those presumptuous people he'd had to deal with...

He remembered the time he'd talked at length to one of Dr. Saunders's colleagues about why he'd been feeling depressed, forcing himself to recall fragments of his past. The professional hadn't really listened to him, insisting that Johnny had been depressed because he'd had a drug problem. Not only was the idea false, but the theory would have also made Johnny a drug-user in grade school. Fortunately, that particular therapist hadn't pushed his hypothesis after Johnny had corrected him.

After catching himself in an unusually and inappropriately deep fit of introspection, especially given his current circumstances, Johnny's attention returned to his immediate surroundings. He realized something: During that whole time, the voice had remained silent, as if letting him recollect things he felt compelled to think about, as much as he didn't want to.

Without forming the words in his mind, Johnny put the past behind him and decided that he didn't have to convince a disembodied voice of anything. He stilled his mind, and could once again sense the underlying compulsion nagging him to shut up, both verbally and mentally.

Listening to the intrusive voice and responding to it with his state of obsessive thought had overpowered and drowned out the seemingly helpful presence inside his head. That helpful presence had been telling him not to listen or respond to the alien voice. He still wasn't sure if the nagging sensation, which was still telling him to tune out the intrusive clutter, was the voice of reason; however, its order for him to ignore the substantial and aggressive voice, which was still urging him to engage it, seemed like a good idea.

He'd have to be more careful.

That was when he heard the voice again:

"There is no world outside of this hospital. I've never seen it."

Johnny refrained from what now seemed to be an attempt to bait him.

"I'll bet you'll try to tell me that you've seen it, though. Am I right?"

Johnny gritted his teeth, trying to clear his head of the disturbance; it was a lot like trying to regain one's balance during a spell of dizziness.

"So, just what do you think you know anyway?"

It was subtle, but Johnny caught a probing sort of undertone in the question, as if it was digging for something more than an anecdotal account to mock.

He didn't need that mysterious and all-too-gentle compulsion to alert him to the fact that this thing was trying to keep Johnny engaged. As tempted as he was to present as much anecdotal evidence about the outside world as he saw fit—if for no other reason than to spite the voice—he obeyed his better judgement and tried to keep himself mentally and verbally quiet.

It now occurred to him that the voice was only putting up a front of being argumentative, perhaps as a means of keeping Johnny's mind open, as well as distracted from the unwelcome speaker's true intentions. He definitely had the feeling that this speaker was trying to extract information that Johnny either wouldn't or couldn't consciously divulge by way of a direct query.

If that were true, his mind had just come dangerously close to being an open lunchbox to something far more threatening than what only seemed to be an obnoxious presence.

Closing his eyes, he forced himself to budge from the spot to reach the column.

The sound of violently bubbling liquid suddenly saturated the room, startling him. He could also hear something akin to hideous muffled gurgling, which, he realized, sounded like innumerable layers of underwater cackling.

Opening his eyes, every creature he could see was indeed trembling inside its tank, making the liquid appear to be boiling.

He didn't know how, but Johnny immediately knew that these things and the voice were connected; they were the ones sending a seemingly-singular antagonist to penetrate his mind. It wasn't just a hypothesis; he knew the beings were controlling the voice, and were trying to break into his mind.

While it confused him to be suddenly aware of the fact, the little guide in his head (or whatever it was prodding him along) had somehow expected this to happen.

(He also had to consider the most unpleasant possibility, which had never ceased to linger in his thoughts: Perhaps he'd become so immersed in his impromptu fantasies that his ability to perceive reality had given up on him entirely. Having come this far, Johnny had to admit that he now preferred real alien surroundings to imaginary ones.)

As if responding to his insight (or delusion), the laughter calmed, and so did the bubbling.

Nervously, he began to tiptoe his way across the room, staying just under a foot away from the left wall. As he did so, he looked between the rows of tanks for a clear path to the base of the column.

The task should have been easy enough, but, after taking his first few steps, he could hear the voice in his head again. This time, however, it wasn't articulating clear words. Its inflections were unnaturally jumbled, too abstract for him to process as anything linguistic.

He could still understand the sentiment driving the intonations, though:

The speaker was aggressively contesting Johnny's capacity to reason, proclaiming its authority on what was true and what wasn't. At the same time, the intruder was also demanding that, if he felt any differently, Johnny would have to prove his case to it... if he wanted it to stay out of his head, anyway.

That last bit had a threatening undertone, its meaning perfectly clear to him: If Johnny didn't let it probe the contents of his mind to the degree of its liking, then the force behind the voice would start to do far more than just pester him.

This thing already knew how to get on his nerves in a way he'd found too overwhelming to ignore, so he didn't doubt that it could find other vulnerabilities in him. Maybe it had already found a few he didn't even know he had, and would surprise him with those findings when he least expected it.

He'd have to avoid thinking about it for now, and just keep going...

Keeping close (but not too close) to the left wall, Johnny strained to tune out the awful sounds in his head. With its sinister cadence and low dips in pitch, the voice became increasingly disturbing to listen to.

He was about halfway across the room when he could finally see the base of the column off to his right. Situated near the centre of the room, he'd have to walk between two rows of tanks to get to it, enduring both the voice and the presence of the creatures facing him from either side.

Johnny drew a long breath and prepared himself for what was going to feel like a mile-long journey.

He'd taken but two steps towards the mouth of the aisle when the voice suddenly split into many, becoming a sea of mental intrusions that made his skin prickle.

All of the creatures in his field of vision began to move more noticeably than before; their breathing deepened and hastened a little, and the slight spasms of their appendages became pronounced twitches, stretches, and wriggling movements. Their eyes began moving about, surveying their surroundings; the ones with eyelids began blinking.

Most of those eyes settled on watching Johnny, following him as he persisted towards the column. In spite of the eyes scrutinizing him, the invasive voices in his head, and his own uneasiness, Johnny managed to keep moving steadily forward.

Startled, he stopped when one of the voices formed something intelligible:

"Where are you going?" it asked innocuously.

Although the words had sounded muffled and as though they'd been gurgled underwater, he knew they'd come from inside his head. Even so, he'd caught a glimpse of a few of the creatures simultaneously opening their orifices and blowing out jets of air, though not quite in time with the syllables.

The question had sounded over layers of continuous peculiar gibberish. He couldn't tell which of the organisms had asked it, or if it had come from the thoughts of one or several of them.

Instead of replying, Johnny continued on his way, trying not to stare back at the abominations staring at him.

"Tell us about yourself," another voice prodded, as if it were mockingly conducting a job interview.

That time, Johnny did catch one of the mouths matching the words with its movements, blowing out a heavy stream of bubbles.

While the vaguely fishlike beast had appeared to be physically speaking, and the voice had sounded as though it were underwater, what he'd actually heard had still come directly from within his mind.

"He is not much like the others here, is he?" asked a different voice, either rhetorically or addressing its counterparts.

"Yes, he is not of this world, I would say," agreed another one, which likely represented a different creature. "If the others' reactions to the conditions here are the norm, this one certainly is not as... disturbed as he should be."

The abstract voices shifted their tone, as if to add their own approval to the idea. The collective expressed their notion with such sincerity that Johnny caught himself actually entertaining the idea that he was profoundly different from other people. (He already knew that he didn't find the situation nearly as troubling as he should have.)

Even though he was trying to ignore them completely, Johnny's mind responded before he could stop it:

"What are you talking about?"

"You are an alien, yes?"

"I'm human," answered Johnny reflexively in his mind, instantly regretting it.

"Well, since you are trying to prove the existence of a fact—this notion of yours that you are human—the burden is on you to convince us that you are native to this world. We do not need to disprove a fact that does not exist; a fact doesn't exist until you convince us it does."

Then, without even offering him time to answer, another of the voices spoke:

"Your tone suggests that you deny our observation. Since you are the one trying to disprove a fact, the burden is on you to convince us that you are not an alien. We do not need to prove what already exists, until you present a convincing argument that refutes it."

Johnny refrained from letting his mind articulate his notice of the loaded statement, that his being an alien was somehow a "fact." Instead, he reminded himself that he hadn't set out to prove anything to anyone.

Besides, he reasoned, how was his being human any less plausible than being an alien from another planet, regardless of which possibility was actually the case?

(Okay, that was a bit crazy, he thought: Did he actually just consider the idea that he wasn't from Earth?)

One argument was trying to put the burden of proof on him, through a rule that he needed to prove an idea when it was voiced in affirmative terms (that he was human). The other argument put the burden of proof on him similarly; however, its rule was that he had the burden of proof because he denied an idea (that he was an alien). While each voice was trying to push the same point, both arguments seemed to focus on the wording of Johnny's next response, specifically whether it would come in positive or negative terms, asserting or denying a claim. As far as he could tell, the only contrast between the approaches came down to semantics; the wording of each argument only changed how he'd respond to what would remain the same point—the point of whether or not he was from another planet.

While neither version of the argument considered his disinterest in proving or refuting anything to anyone, both of them served to put Johnny in the same defensive position while making the presupposed and wild claim that he was an alien.

He'd heard some shoddy technicalities used to push ideas on him before, but this... Their line of reasoning came across as a slightly bent version of something similar he'd heard a few times in the past...

"Let us try this again," began the voices, "A negative claim cannot be proven. Therefore, our assertion of the negative—that you are not human—is not for us to prove.

"So, you are responsible for proving the positive assertion that you are human.... if indeed you are. Keep in mind that, until you prove the existence of a fact, that fact in question does not exist."

Johnny didn't know why he was surprised to hear them parroting that familiar philosophy verbatim. Without thinking, he just went ahead and indulged them with a response. "You're saying that a negative can't be proven, just because it's a negative? That sure covers a lot of different negatives…

"So, if I say that there is no creature living under my bed, I can't prove the point by getting a flashlight and then taking a looksee under the mattress? Do you mean to tell me that all negative claims are equally unprovable, just because they are negative? You don't think other factors, like hard evidence or deductive reasoning, affect even the likelihood of a negative claim; you know, the way they tend to affect a positive one?"

There was no answer.

Johnny wondered how many people only resorted to this blanket-rule on a selective basis, while they remained willing to prove negative claims when it was convenient. "I don't have to back up my claim because it's a negative claim," came off as a technicality, a cheap and lazy tactic to get out of qualifying the assertion with an actual argument.

Johnny couldn't say why he or anyone would refuse to actually look under that hypothetical bed to confirm the creature's nonexistence. He imagined that some people might if they were extremely stubborn, or afraid of what they would find down there. Perhaps they had a bad back, or believed that getting down on their hands and knees was beneath them.

Really, why was someone's burden of proof eliminated the moment his or her statement became difficult or impossible to prove; or, supposedly impossible to prove because it had been voiced in negative terms? The concept seemed like an excuse to transfer the burden of proof to anyone making a positive counterclaim. Meanwhile, the one making that positive counterclaim was never exempt from that burden under any circumstances…

Sardonically, Johnny supposed the lesson to be learned from this way of thinking was that one should always make sure to voice one's opinions in negative terms.

He grew suspicious of those who resorted to face-value rules like that, especially when those same people were likely to put words in his mouth, as if to lend credence to their point. For instance, contrary to the accusations of such individuals, Johnny didn't recall ever having said to them, "Because you can't disprove the possibility of my positive assertion, then my positive assertion is automatically and irrefutably true."

In fact, if he remembered correctly, they were the ones who often made childish assertions like, "Because you can't immediately prove your point in positive terms—to a degree of my liking—then my denial of it is automatically correct." In other words, "If I don't see anything outside my field of vision, then it simply doesn't exist, period."

As if in response to Johnny's ponderings, or the heated agitation they were generating, the voices cut into his mind with a unanimous burst of derisive laughter.

Johnny stopped himself from answering the taunt. As it was, he'd already engaged the voices after resolving not to, and he was about to do it again. Instead, he mentally reaffirmed his disinterest in responding to his psychological adversaries (who could have been figments of his imagination); or, at least, he reaffirmed the disinterest he should have had in even examining what the creatures were trying to do.

Yet, as all the voices were now just shouting their overbearing abstractions of language at him—which insisted he couldn't trust anything he thought he understood about himself—his mind instinctively drank what it was given, processing it.

Staring at the column while taking step after step towards it, he fought the natural urge to reflect on the intrusions he couldn't stop automatically processing, as if by reflex.

It was like seeing a ferocious animal, the existence of which you intuitively knew you weren't supposed to acknowledge; some mythical beast that would be drawn to you the moment you had any thoughts about its appearance or behaviour, or even acquired a mental description of it.

Finally, Johnny's mind impassively humoured the dominant disturbance without agreement or disagreement:

"So, you think I'm not human."

"Who said anything about being human? You are an alien to us," murmured a cluster of voices in Johnny's head.

Now, that was just moving the goal posts! He really couldn't stand it when people redefined a concept in mid-conversation as a sneaky way to retroactively change the subject, revising their point to dodge arguments and confuse him.

"Besides, you know you do not fit in with other people," chorused another contingent of countless voices in unison. "You are different from other people, or, 'alien,' to be technical."

Changing their meaning of the word "alien" yet again, he didn't doubt that they were trying to obfuscate and derail any consistent line of reasoning that Johnny could respond with (even though he was still struggling to keep himself from answering with anything clear).

With his mind busily trying to remain calm in the midst of the mental uproar, he hadn't immediately noticed that the shaft was now right in front of him. The strain on him had made the trip feel like it had taken hours; although he'd walked slowly, it had probably only taken a few minutes.

Staring at the surface of metallic green, which was just three feet away from him, he found that the voices were now marginally easier to ignore. Unsure of why he'd prodded himself towards this thing, Johnny began circling it warily, while staying as far from the surrounding tanks as possible.

On the opposite side of the towering cylinder—the side he'd approached initially—there was a smooth silvery door set into its surface. Looking as though it slid open sideways, Johnny surmised that the column was an elevator, offering access to the walkways above.

Taking a step closer to the door, he looked around it for any buttons or panels…

The gentle chime of a bell startled Johnny before the door began to slide open silently. He took a step back, and his mind raced frantically to find some impromptu explanation for why he was here. He winced as the inside of the lift fully revealed itself.

To his sudden relief, no shocked or disapproving faces greeted him from within the empty compartment.

As peculiar as it was, Johnny deduced that the elevator must have been automatic, its door meant to open welcomingly to anyone who came in its proximity. In light of the unusual things about this whole place, he considered that this was still far from the oddest one.

Still a little unnerved from his momentary scare, though also anxious to get on with whatever he was supposed to do, Johnny entered the open compartment.

# Chapter 7

LETTING THE ELEVATOR DOOR slide shut behind him, Johnny looked around the steely cylindrical interior a moment. He couldn't spot any buttons or even lights in here, though he could see perfectly.

He was surprised to notice the sudden absence of voices in his head. There was only the gentle intuitive guide reassuring him that he was on the right track.

He hadn't had five seconds of peace before the floor gave a sudden jerk, followed by the brief gentle sensation of his body being pulled downward. While he hoped his senses weren't giving him a false impression of ascending the shaft, Johnny also dreaded whatever he would find once that door opened again (if it opened again).

Feeling another downward pull, Johnny swallowed slowly as he watched the door move aside to reveal the maze of suspended walkways he'd seen from below. From what he could observe up here, nothing was connecting the pathways to the ceiling high above. Keeping in mind that there was nothing holding them aloft from below either, he wondered how it was possible for such heavy-looking materials to float in midair, as if by magic.

He also wondered if setting foot on the floor outside the elevator would be safe.

A few of the walkways were barricaded and partially concealed by thick walls that stood some eight feet high; they were made of the same exotic green material covering the walls of the chamber. Most of the walkways, however, had little more than a low black railing to serve as a barrier, which was hardly enough to alleviate his fear of losing his footing and plummeting to the floor below.

The paths themselves had the same glossy black surface that the floor below did, though here they looked wet, as if they were slippery. Then again, considering how far down the main floor was, Johnny's perception might have been exaggerating the appearance of any potentially unsafe conditions.

The sum of the diverging and converging walkways and walls made for quite a confusing mess to look at. Taking a minute to study the many paths, he noticed that every turn he could see was a forty-five degree angle.

There were also several open doorways—or perhaps door-shaped alcoves—on each of the chamber walls. He could see only a couple of feet into the nearest opening before all trace of light suddenly ceased.

Whether they were passageways or deep alcoves, each of them was bridged to the network of pathways. He couldn't see any direct route from where he was standing to any of the recesses, which could have been exits. Even without walls interrupting his view, the many exposed walkways were overwhelming to look at, and the very thought of traversing them made him feel disoriented.

Nevertheless, Johnny obeyed his mental guide and timidly stepped out of the lift and onto the floor.

In spite of its appearance, it seemed to have enough traction to walk on safely.

Proceeding carefully, Johnny traversed the walkways, making his best guess when choosing to turn this way or that in order to get to the nearest opening.

To his increasing frustration and despair, his mental guide wasn't acting as a compass to direct him through this place, or giving him even a subtle indication of which passageway he should try to reach.

As time went on, Johnny could have sworn that the layout of the maze had changed several times, seeming bigger and more complex with every alteration. The experience was actually making him feel dizzy and a little sick to his stomach.

Worse still, after Johnny had finally reached one of the openings and stepped through it, he found himself walking out of an identical opening in less than five paces, facing what seemed to be the same chamber he'd just exited. While reason dictated that he must have entered a different area, he couldn't shake the perception of having entered the opposite side of the same chamber through one of the other openings.

Johnny compelled himself to travel the maze again and look for the real way out, if there was one. He did his best to ignore the feeling that the effort was pointless because there was no escaping this place. There was no way to know how much time he'd spent wandering around, entering one passage and exiting another in what seemed to be the same chamber.

Returning to the elevator by chance had confirmed what he'd already suspected:

The door wouldn't open automatically, and, with no way of forcing it open, he was stuck up here.

Feeling flushed and light-headed, sickly and exhausted, he'd bumped into a wall at least a couple of times. After he'd found himself nearly tipping over a railing (which gave his heart quite a jump), he decided to sit on the floor, close his eyes, and rest a moment. Hopefully, the fit of vertigo would pass...

Not a minute later, a voice suddenly bellowed in his head, propelling Johnny to his feet:

"Why are you trying to leave?" it demanded. "How can you believe that you are fit to believe anything if you cannot say anything to convince us otherwise?"

Ignoring the words, Johnny resumed what was going to be an aimless and desperate attempt to get out of this maze.

"You are not unwilling to prove yourself; you are unable," it taunted.

Clenching his jaw, Johnny stumbled along the walkways in haste, though trying to be careful and keep his balance.

Meanwhile, layers of distorted babble returned to fill his mind with abstract taunts. Periodically, coherent words joined in the mental assault, some of which clearer than others:

"Prove to us that you are not standing on the ceiling."

"Prove to us that you are standing on any kind of floor."

"Prove that you are not just floating in a tank like the rest of us. Otherwise, you are just imagining that you are walking around outside."

"Explain yourself in terms we can understand, or you do not know what you are talking about."

"Do it now!"

"Are you getting upset? You are too sensitive; remember your anxiety attacks?"

That struck a nerve.

"What, so you're suggesting that I'm incapable of saying anything reasonably credible or of significant value?" he asked aloud, in spite of himself.

"Nothing you have said or could ever say has any credibility or value whatsoever."

Another of the voices changed the topic:

"Do you realize that you have just spent the past few hours trying to argue with voices in your head, imagining that sleeping beings in tanks are talking to you?"

"You seem awake to me," Johnny's mind muttered back reflexively. Meanwhile, he paused his frantic tottering to prop himself against a nearby wall.

Though he hadn't sought to think it, he had to admit to himself that it was strange to be more upset about the content of the mental intrusions than his other circumstances, including the fact his mind was being invaded at all.

"Are you sure that the creatures are awake, let alone aware of you? You are not in a position to make rational observations," one of the speakers replied with condescension.

"Nutjob," added another voice, emphasizing the antipathy in its counterpart's remark.

Between the overpowering barrage of mental assaults and the layout up here, Johnny couldn't stand it anymore. His anger shot through the roof, quickly overpowering every other emotion. Soon after, the rush of adrenaline escalated it into ferocity. Unable to hold back what he hadn't even realized he'd been holding back for so long, he experienced the first feeling of wanting to hit someone (that he could consciously remember) since being institutionalized.

Then, as quickly as his rage had enflamed, something else in his mind seized it, transmuting it into something else before he could act:

Johnny, feeling a fit of light-headed giddiness, let out the longest raspberry he'd ever given anyone.

The voices spoke to him in unison, their tone menacingly pleased:

"So, that is one of your secrets. Tell us, what other little things about yourself are you trying to hide?"

Johnny didn't need to think much about the voices' meaning, as he immediately understood what had just happened, namely what "secret" they'd been referring to:

The real cause of his impulsive, childlike state—why it came and went—had indeed been a secret. In fact, keeping it a secret had been so crucial that, until now, Johnny had kept it hidden from himself.

Fortunately, Johnny's understanding of what the creatures now understood had also interrupted the onset of what would have been another fit of regression.

Unfortunately, his ability to understand had largely come from what the voices conveyed about their own comprehension of his mental workings. Delivering their insights through a form of virtual telepathy, what they knew about him was ingrained in their non-language, gibberish to the ears.

While studying his mind from within, they'd just witnessed one of his mood swings from an intimate perspective. Having analyzed it, they were now triumphantly reflecting their findings back into Johnny's consciousness, reminding him of what he'd needed to forget.

No doubt they were trying to jog his memory so it would be prompted to reveal even more to them.

Johnny wouldn't think about how, before coming to the hospital, he'd trained his mind to enter that childlike rambunctious state. He wouldn't think about how he'd also trained himself to forget training himself, which, even then, he'd known would create certain necessary risks:

There was the risk of losing focus at the worst possible time, which would put him and the mission in danger, and also the risk of losing his unconscious control over when and for how long the mental regression would stay active. There was also a chance that the self-induced state would act capriciously, failing to become active when the situation needed it to be, or, worse still, become active at the worst possible times.

He tried not to think about it.

"Too late," announced the voices, gloating. "We know all about it; even what was supposed to trigger that little quirk of yours. You know what that trigger is, don't you?"

They already knew the answer to that.

He'd known the moment he'd felt that surge of hostility, which was the trigger.

It wasn't just irritability or anger; Johnny had to feel enraged beyond his control, experiencing the boiling point of becoming physically violent.

Feeling that way, never mind acting on it, was dangerous here. Because he'd been aware of that well before his arrival to the sanatorium, he'd somehow managed to program himself to channel that emotional energy into something less… damaging.

"To us or yourself?" asked the voices sardonically. Without their actually making the sound, Johnny could still hear their virtual laughter.

Why couldn't he get his brain to shut up? These things already knew too much!

Johnny disregarded his sense of self for a moment, and, turning his attention to the network of walkways, imagined that he was a rat about to run through a maze.

"Oh, and we so wanted to learn more about this mission of yours," said the voices with mock lament.

Johnny could almost hear them smiling mischievously. Focusing on nothing but the maze, and vividly picturing himself as a small furry rodent, he began to think of finding a piece of cheese.

"Suit yourself," said the voices, as if suddenly deciding to give up. "Alien."

Their backing off made Johnny snap out of his reverie, leaving him a little taken aback and suspicious: Surely, the speakers couldn't have been finished with him yet… Much to his surprise, however, every trace of their voices had finally departed from his mind's ear, which had been hearing them in stereo.

Looking again at the many routes around him, Johnny was also astonished to immediately perceive the way to each of the doorways. He felt as though his senses had just been flushed of something that had been clogging them; something he hadn't even known was there.

He was past the point of apprehension, now. Not about to get choosy on the matter of which doorway he would try next, Johnny hurried to the nearest one, and stepped through it.

As long as it didn't lead back to the chamber, he didn't care where he ended up.

As it turned out, he ended up in the big front lobby of a hospital building, with a wide reception desk ten paces ahead of him. To the left of it, further back, he could see part of a cafeteria; its counters, tables, and chairs were on a raised platform overlooking the rest of the floor.

Thick lines of people moved silently in either direction across the floor, seamlessly flowing between him and the reception desk. Walking absently, half of them emerged from the left passage only to disappear down the right, while the rest moved in the opposite direction. He could see visitors, doctors, nurses, interns, patients, and even a few caretakers; no one acted any differently from the next person. Their eyes appeared vacant, which added to the look of utter obliviousness they had about them; Johnny was surprised that these people weren't bumping into one another.

Fortunately, the quiet passers-by also seemed to be unaware of Johnny as they mechanically sauntered along.

To his immediate left, a security desk sat abandoned, and to his right, the entrance to a small flower shop was barred shut.

Turning around slowly, Johnny saw a row of automatic glass doors marking the hospital's front entrance. In theory, that had been the way through which he'd entered the lobby. Gazing through the panes, he could tell that daylight still wasn't coming any time soon. From where he was standing, he could also make out streetlights, a road busy with passing cars, and a row of buildings across it.

This wasn't the side of the hospital that faced the other buildings in the compound; this was the side that faced civilization. All he had to do to complete his escape was go through one of those doors and keep walking (while making sure a car didn't hit him).

That guiding sense in his head had a different idea, which coupled with his underlying reservations about trying to leave: The row of doors were probably only there to fool him into thinking he could just walk outside and leave the compound with ease. If recent memory could be relied on (now he wasn't so sure about that), wouldn't he just end up back in that big green room?

He'd probably just find himself in yet another place, even more alien than before, he thought bitterly.

Johnny couldn't trust his senses anymore (if he ever really could). If he wasn't prone to hallucinations, then the structure of the world around him was unreliable, bending and twisting to emotionally and psychologically cripple him.

To think: All he had to do was see one clear picture of civilization to drive home the feeling that he would never see the real thing again. If he did, he doubted he would ever truly believe that it was the real thing.

Taking a few seconds to wallow in self-pity, Johnny felt his eyes beginning to sting with the onset of tears. His guiding sense wanted him to move away from the exit, whether or not it actually led outside. Knowing that it probably didn't, Johnny resigned himself to his instinctive pull to proceed deeper into the hospital.

His intuitive guide decided that he should join one of the streams of people moving down the left passage, so he unhappily obeyed. Passing a gift shop, doors, elevators, and a couple of vending machines, Johnny noticed that the crowd was gradually thinning out. While there were plenty of corridors offering access to the other sections of the hospital, he continued down the main passage, which eventually turned right.

This hallway had no windows or doors, and was rather dark. Still, the spotless beige walls and thick brown carpeting reassured him that he hadn't wandered his way into the Hole.

After passing through an open doorway at the end of the short hall, Johnny had to slow down to get his bearings.

# Chapter 8

JOHNNY WASN'T SURE if he'd just entered another hallway, or a chamber. Stretching out over forty feet ahead of him, this empty section was maybe twenty feet wide. The soft carpeting that covered both the floor and the upper half of the walls was an eyesore. Long asymmetrical splotches of dark red were set against a background of navy blue, which made for a design that was nauseating to look upon.

The bulbs in the ceiling fixtures were dim, some of them flickering. The irregular and scant lighting made the carpeting harder to look at, while the flickering also brought miserable memories of the Hole to mind.

For some reason, he now felt as though he'd travelled thousands of miles away from another living soul to an isolated section of the hospital. However, the sounds of distant human activity were definitely audible; the flow of overlapping footsteps and conversations were coming from behind him. (He found that a little odd; he hadn't heard any of those sounds moments ago, when he'd been in the middle of the very crowd that was probably making them.)

Fighting feelings of desolation, dread, and a touch of vertigo, Johnny fought to continue onward.

Johnny wasn't sure if his sudden heavy-heartedness was just a natural progression of his existing unhappy mood, or if there was something specific about this place that had so radically intensified his feeling of hopelessness, and of being utterly alone.

He had to admit, he'd never felt nearly as depressed as he did the moment he'd realized the futility of simply walking out of the hospital and into the city, which had been right in front of him. (His ranking of depressing moments included all the times he'd been locked in his quarters for hours, left alone with his thoughts.)

If the appearance of his surroundings were hallucinations, maybe they did reflect his mood. Maybe, even if the world around him were the product of a waking dream, it could still exaggerate or elicit feelings that he wouldn't have otherwise experienced of his own accord. He imagined one part of his consciousness leaving his head just so it could be assimilated back into it, creating sensations that might as well have come from a sensory stimulus that was separate from him.

The décor was really disgusting to look at; maybe that was all there was to his worsening mood. Even if it really did exist in the objective world—and not in his head—he couldn't tell if it was something that was normally here or if it was another transitory rearrangement of reality. He had to consider that, when it came to aesthetics, people in the real world could have some pretty tacky ideas of what looked good.

Johnny let out an involuntary sigh of disgust; even when he was at his emotional lowest, barely caring about what was really going on, he still couldn't stop his ongoing attempts to analyze things that were likely beyond his capacity to grasp.

Even after approaching what he would have thought was the halfway point of the hideous floor, the far wall and the open doorway at the end of it seemed no closer to him than it had been when he'd first entered this section. He also could have sworn that the splotches on the carpeting were moving, floating about the blue background and gradually changing shape while remaining separate from one another.

Of course, what he was seeing now could have come from a combination of exhaustion and terrible lighting playing with his eyes.

There really was no point in straining to figure out the cause of every little thing he was experiencing. As it was, extreme lethargy was making his every step a monumental task.

"I am so sick of this," he muttered despairingly as he closed his eyes,

127

now stumbling along blindly.

Not long after making the complaint, Johnny felt a vertical flat surface bump against his head, and the rest of his body shortly thereafter.

Opening his eyes, Johnny was marginally pleased to see that he was now on the far side of the room, facing its wall and an exit just a couple of steps to his right.

Leaving the ugly room behind, Johnny began an absent walk down another hall with clean beige walls, brown carpeting on the floor, and lighting that was soft, but stable. As his thoughts melted into a heap of incoherence, his eyes began to glaze over while his legs remained in motion.

Without noticing the transition, Johnny found himself walking atop thick red carpeting, down a hallway lined with numbered wooden doors. He'd never seen faded gold wallpaper used in a hospital before, which probably meant that his immediate environment was playing another trick on him.

The few people that were walking towards and past him hadn't seemed to notice anything odd or out of place, though they'd appeared too distracted to notice much of anything.

The hallway led to what looked like a ritzy hotel lobby, which he neither found surprising nor disturbing. Now, the sight of something out of place was just tiresome and depressing.

The carpet was still red, while white streaks covered the otherwise loud pink wallpaper.

Wearily, he tottered in, seeing an unmanned reception desk to his left. Two elevator doors were situated in the wall behind the desk; one to either side of it. To his right, there was a wide staircase with ornate black handrails offering access to the floor above. Just ahead of him, in the centre of the room, a group of men in tuxedos were sitting on black leather sofas, which were positioned in a loose circle around a wooden coffee table.

The gentlemen appeared to be cheerily talking amongst themselves, and yet Johnny couldn't hear even the slightest peep coming from any of them. They hadn't noticed him, either, which he supposed was good.

Normally, wearing his white pyjamas and slippers in such a formal and posh atmosphere would have made him feel awkwardly conspicuous. (His getting snubbed certainly wasn't going to offend him in any case, what with his being on the run and all.)

Now, however, he was too despondent to worry about what he was seeing anymore, too tired to grapple with the question of whether or not every aspect of the group actually existed. Still, a part of him wondered if these men were total hallucinations, or real people his hallucinations had modified. Perhaps these guys were hospital patients or visitors, which his deranged imagination had remade into antiquated archetypes of high society.

Had it not been for his guiding sense, Johnny probably would have resigned himself to a vegetable state back in the hospital lobby. However, maintaining any confidence in that quiet little guide in his head was also getting wearisome (although his level of confidence in it had been pretty shaky to begin with). Still, he had nothing else to give him any sense of direction or a reason to act, so he'd have to continue humouring his latent impulses until his will to keep going was finally extinguished.

"That shouldn't take too long," he lamented, muttering the sentiment aloud.

The gentlemen turned to face Johnny and smiled at him deviously.

Then, without waiting for Johnny to react, one of the men rose from his seat and, as if producing them from under his sleeve, offered Johnny a piece of paper and a long, black quill.

Accepting the paper reluctantly, he left the pen in the hand of the mischievously-grinning man, who kept it outstretched. Johnny looked over the paper, and frowned:

Except for an area near the bottom of the page that was clearly meant for his signature, the document was illegible. Though he could plainly see characters in black ink, they were either really sloppily handwritten or they were from an alphabet he'd never seen before. (Maybe the letters were both clumsily scrawled and from an alphabet he didn't recognize.)

"Will you please sign?" asked the gentleman in a smarmy voice.

"What is this?" asked Johnny, narrowing his eyes as he looked over the inky mess of gibberish covering the page.

"It's a contract," replied one of the man's associates from his seat.

Johnny let out an exasperated sigh. "What's in it?"

"Just sign it," insisted the man with the quill, maintaining his friendly air. The others reinforced the pushy recommendation with a nod.

"I don't even know what I'm signing, or, really, why I'm even being given a contract," replied Johnny, his tone sounding a little whinier than he'd wanted it to. "What is this?" he demanded, waving the paper at the grinning dork with the quill.

"Why, it's whatever you think it is. Just sign it and trust us."

Johnny squinted his eyes in disbelief, as his mind was taken back to ugly memories of dodgy people.

"How can I trust or distrust what you refuse to explain? You just want me to blindly accept... something, whatever this crap supposedly says," said Johnny, as he irritably shook the paper with one hand before smacking it with the other.

"Just take it as a given that we have the intentions that you would expect us to have, especially if you were in our position," replied the fraudster with the quill. "We shouldn't need to tell you these things."

"What does any of that mean; what intentions? You haven't even asked me about what I expect from you, and you have no way of knowing what that is... How can I assume you have my expectations in mind if you're not even saying aloud what you think they are?" asked Johnny, barking the question.

Johnny knew how this game of theirs worked: Some people liked to evade specifying their intentions towards you so they wouldn't be called liars when they violated whatever implicit terms they still wanted you to believe they would honour. They wouldn't state good intentions or any intentions at all, while hoping that you'd trust the assumptions they wanted you to make.

After misleading you, it was easy for them to resort to that tired, old technical excuse: They hadn't outright broken any spelled-out promises, and you should have known better than to make assumptions about their intentions.

"My, aren't we closed-minded," chided the entire group collectively.

There was something awfully familiar about the way these men were interacting with Johnny. Actually, it was reminiscent of how the creatures in their tanks had taken to arguing with him not too long ago; and, just like the last time, his latest antagonists' attempts to provoke and distract him were working.

Much to his annoyance, his awareness of getting swept up in an unwelcome exchange, which he should have been avoiding, had come a little late.

He had to fight to make sure he didn't take anything they said at face value.

Even so, their shaming tactic of trying to blackmail him intellectually had struck a nerve:

"There's nothing closed-minded about calling out a fraud," he muttered through his clenched teeth. "Besides, if I were to accept everything you throw at me in the name of 'open-mindedness,' then I would never get to apply whatever lessons real open-mindedness could teach me. If I can't apply what I learn, then there's no point to learning anything…

"If there's no point to learning anything, then, even if I were being closed-minded, there's no point to having any degree of open-mindedness… let alone whatever kind of submissive stupidity you're expecting from me."

While the words flowed smoothly out of his mouth, Johnny could feel his body beginning to shake a little with aggression. He'd already been deep in a foul mood before getting subjected to this.

What he heard next sounded like a caricatured paraphrasing of the shaming tactics he'd heard manipulative people use whenever they wanted to get their way:

"Why don't you just show us that you're a smart, trusting person who doesn't act like a coward when facing risks?"

Yes, Johnny thought: He should stupidly pander to the notion that these people needed to be convinced of anything in order for it to be valid. He should do the "brave" thing and indulge them out of an insecurity of being called insecure.

Even though he knew he should have ignored the taunt, Johnny really couldn't stop himself from thinking about the vile and manipulative mentality that it represented.

Then, bearing his teeth, Johnny belligerently tore up the paper, crumpled its pieces into a ball, and flung it past the man with the quill, towards his seated associates.

As he watched it bounce off the head of one of them, who didn't even flinch, Johnny realized something:

This time, he didn't feel any sign of an emerging regressive fit to hold back, which maybe should have been disconcerting. Right now, he was too wound up to care.

Something distracted the entire group just then; as the self-satisfied company made a synchronized turn in the direction of the reception desk, a shared look of terror replaced their smirks.

Johnny turned his head to see what they were looking at; the nearest elevator (or perhaps both elevators) had been the cause of their alarm. While Johnny focused on the elevators and the desk between them, he could see the group darting away out of the corner of his eye.

By the time he looked back at the couches, everyone was gone, including the man with the quill. They hadn't fled in the direction of the stairs; the only other visible way out of the room was through the passage behind him, and they'd moved in the opposite direction.

Since they were either concoctions of his ever-externalized imagination or creations of his unstable surroundings, Johnny supposed he shouldn't have been terribly surprised that they could just disappear within a fraction of a second, as if escaping into nothingness.

Without making a sound, the elevator doors opened simultaneously, revealing a broad-shouldered human figure standing within each compartment. The two identical men were covered from head to toe in charcoal-grey armour that looked extremely cumbersome.

Simultaneously, they stepped into the room and stopped to look around, as if searching for something.

Hoping they wouldn't notice him if he didn't move, Johnny stood perfectly still. He took in their menacing appearance, which erased every trace of the hostility that had been surging through him just seconds ago.

Both figures must have been close to seven feet tall. The plating that covered their bodies appeared thick and heavy, though Johnny doubted that there were gangly little men beneath. Johnny wasn't sure if each suit's semi-reflective pieces were metallic or they'd been cut from something organic, like the exoskeleton of a giant insect. In fact, the shape of the uniform reminded him a little of a beetle that could walk upright on two legs. A reflective plate covered the face of its heavy-looking helmet, bringing to mind a convex mirror.

Johnny couldn't identify the origin of the outfit; checking its vest and helmet, he could see nothing resembling a flag, badge, or insignia of any kind. The seemingly standard-issue attire didn't belong to any police force or military on Earth that he could think of.

Still, the men's armour seemed a little familiar, though the mirror-covered faces seemed a little out of place. As intimidating as these two were to behold, their presence also brought a feeling that was strangely nostalgic, and perhaps a little reassuring.

Perhaps he'd seen these guys, or at least what they were wearing, in a science fiction movie when he was a kid, and the world around him had pulled the latent memory out of his head to show it to him.

Whether they were supposed to be soldiers or guards, Johnny supposed he should have been glad that neither of them appeared to be carrying rifles, or any other weapons. However, neither of them looked like they would need firearms of any kind to deal with whatever came their way.

For a fleeting moment, Johnny hoped his perception was twisting the forms to look the way they did; perhaps they were really just janitors, or little old ladies.

It didn't take long for them to notice him; when they did, neither moved from his respective spot. They eased their rigid posture, and looked at him, almost as though they were expecting him to do or say something.

As dangerous as they seemed, Johnny raised his hands in a gesture of surrender and braved taking a few slow steps towards them.

Both of them raised an arm in what looked like a military-style salute, which startled Johnny, prompting him to pause with his hands still raised. Tilting his head, he beseeched them for an explanation with a confused look.

They said nothing in response, maintaining their rigidly respectful pose, as if waiting for him to do or say something.

Rather nervously, Johnny tried addressing them, albeit meekly:

"Uh... At ease?"

They lowered their arms, but didn't appear any more relaxed than before. Then again, Johnny couldn't imagine them in any state that wasn't formal or robotic. He had to wonder what was beneath those helmets...

Johnny tensed as the two stepped towards him, even though their gait was non-threatening.

Unable to blink, his eyes remained fixed on the mirror covering the nearest soldier's face as it came within a foot of his own, tilting downward as though its owner wanted to scrutinize him threateningly. Staring into it, Johnny stopped seeing his reflection and instead began to perceive his own face behind a transparent surface.

Dismissing the trick that his mind must have been playing on him, Johnny looked away from the helmet and tried taking a step back. Neither of the large men seemed to have a problem with it, so Johnny took another backwards step, and then another...

Neither of the men moved from his spot, though Johnny had the sense that he was still being watched closely. Once he could feel the railing of the stairs pressing into his back, he chanced turning around.

Before even thinking about it, he made a hasty ascent to the next floor; he sprinted up the first set of wide stairs to the landing and scrambled his way up the second on all fours.

Absently, he opened a door at the top of the staircase and crossed the threshold. In a daze of exhaustion, he turned right and began jogging down yet another long hallway with beige walls, brown carpeting, and low lighting. He couldn't see any end to the passage ahead, though there were plenty of closed doors on either wall; something about them gave him the impression that they were decorative, and wouldn't actually open.

While in a bit of a stupor, Johnny wondered how long this building could possibly be, since he'd been travelling in this same direction for what seemed like forever. Perhaps this building didn't have finite dimensions, and his own demented mind had led him into a place where he'd be trapped for eternity.

He wasn't sure if that guiding sense was now pushing him along, or if his mind had grown so numb that it was simply easier for him to mindlessly continue onward than it was to stop and make any conscious decisions.

To his surprise, he wasn't getting tired from the long jog. Sure, his mental and emotional burdens were certainly draining his energy, and thus affecting his body; the physical activity of non-stop motion didn't seem to be contributing to the strain he was feeling. Actually, he couldn't remember breaking into a sweat even once all night. Although he was still in motion now, he had yet to feel himself perspire.

In a mental haze, Johnny thought about the last time he'd had a drink of water, or used the bathroom, and he realized that he couldn't remember the last time he'd felt the need to do either of those things. Sure, he remembered having done both during his stay at the sanatorium, but not at all this evening or earlier today.

Even in the past, such activities had been rare. They had only been carried out in response to his circumstances. Whenever he'd been brought food and drink, he'd responded by eating and drinking. Meanwhile, using the bathroom had been merely a part of his daily routine. He couldn't recall actually having felt thirsty or the urge to pee since becoming a patient at the mental hospital.

Johnny needed to slow down to think about this.

When he did, however, he quickly forgot what it was that he'd wanted to think about, after suddenly noticing a tall dark figure keeping pace with him to either side. He wasn't sure if these were the same soldiers he'd seen downstairs, or these were two more who'd somehow snuck up on him from out of nowhere.

Of course, there was still no way of knowing for sure if the intimidating men were real. So far, they were just walking alongside him; they weren't doing anything to hinder or harm him, so he supposed he would quietly humour their presence for now.

His thoughts now focused exclusively on the mysterious pair of escorts, Johnny wondered if they were here to protect him or if they saw him as their prisoner. Feeling uneasy about saying anything to them, never mind asking them questions, Johnny only observed their manner as the three of them proceeded along the seemingly endless hallway.

Whenever he hastened his pace, they hastened their pace. Whenever he slowed down, they slowed down. If Johnny sped up too quickly and got even a couple of feet ahead of them, both would hurry past him; without moving right in front of him, they would then extend their arms in his path, making the silent statement that he wasn't allowed to get too far away from them.

Even if they were there to protect him, Johnny doubted they would respect any attempt he made to decline their assistance.

Before Johnny could process it, the hallway changed again:

The three of them were slowly proceeding down a narrow tunnel with surfaces covered in shiny metal plating that resembled a light coffee-coloured copper. The low ceiling, no more than a foot above his head, bore tiny amber-coloured lights, which lit the area gently, but thoroughly and evenly.

The two soldiers repositioned themselves right behind him, since there wasn't room for all three of them to walk alongside one another; the floor was no more than five feet across. It was also covered with grating, which appeared to be made of the same metal that covered the walls and ceiling.

Looking through the grid, Johnny could make out the shapes of pipes and wires a few feet down, as well as a few blinking orange and red lights.

The octagonal shape of the passage and the sound of trickling water up ahead brought to mind a high-tech conduit of some sort, or at least something deep underground. He could also hear what sounded like a low electronic hum filling the air, possibly originating from behind the walls.

Beginning to think that he was in a top-secret research or military facility, the long corridor also made Johnny imagine that he was inside of a futuristic submarine, space station, or a construction that wasn't even built on Earth. Wherever and whatever this place was, something about its character matched that of the two soldiers, who were still walking uncomfortably close to him.

While moving further down the corridor, he noticed the occasional recess in either wall. All of them had the size and shape of a doorway, though what they contained varied. Some were empty, flat coppery walls, while others housed panels, which bore handles and looked removable, perhaps concealing machinery. Without stopping to inspect it, he noticed a small terminal in one of the indentations to his left; a low console comprised of a black screen, keyboard, as well as other miscellaneous buttons and switches. Other alcoves contained heavy-looking doors, the metal of which was a little darker in tone than the surrounding interior.

On the right side of each door, he noticed a small keypad, which triggered an impulse for him to do something. His guiding sense dispelled the urge as quickly as it had come, as if telling him that he had the right idea, but the wrong keypad.

For all he knew, even with a corresponding keypad, each of the doors could have been an imitation of the real thing or a product of his imagination... like this entire area could have been.

Further along, vending machines and automatic coffee dispensers, foam cups and all, sat to either side of the passage. Each device occupied its own recess, appearing intermittently between the doors and empty alcoves.

That couldn't have been right, he thought; if the entirety of his surroundings weren't out of sorts, then either the dispensers or everything else around them didn't belong here. Yet, as much as Johnny tried to believe that, he couldn't be sure. Maybe there really was a contrasting mess of mundane and unusual things in here; maybe someone had deliberately designed this place to look the way it did in order to keep any passers-through confused.

The guide in his head chased off his worries about where he really was and what he was supposed to be doing. It insisted that he shouldn't panic or allow anything to distract or deter him. If this strange form of intuition was accurate in the slightest, then Johnny was extremely close to whatever it thought his goal was supposed to be.

Now, every twenty paces or so, his path through the corridor was making abrupt diagonal turns to the left and right, though he and his companions were still travelling in the same general direction. The layout of each section between turns yielded not only recesses in the same places, but the same variety of objects (or lack thereof) within them.

Sometimes, he'd find a coffee machine where there'd been a door in the previous corridor, or a panel where there'd been a terminal, but it wasn't long before Johnny began to second-guess the exact order of the things he'd seen along the previous stretch. He refrained from going back to make sure that he wasn't walking down the exact same corridor over and over again. As he advanced, he could hear that perpetual watery trickle getting louder, which was enough to reassure him that he was making progress.

After a few minutes of continuing his steady and determined walk, Johnny eventually saw where the sound of flowing water was coming from:

In a low recess at the far end of the corridor, there was what looked like a reflective black drinking fountain protruding from the wall behind. To the right of the fountain in front of him, the passage continued diagonally rightward.

Approaching the object slowly, while periodically glancing down the adjacent corridor, Johnny inspected the object.

It had the shape of a small toilet, and brought to mind his earlier thoughts about drinking and bathroom activities. The hybrid of a drinking fountain and a toilet actually looked a little like a miniature bidet. Appalled at the idea of using the device for any of the purposes that it brought to mind, Johnny was also sure that it wouldn't normally exist here, and that it had materialized as a result of his conscious musings.

Something in this place, or this place itself, was reading his mind and injecting aspects of it into the real world. That must have been what it was...

Then again, perhaps that influence, whatever its source, was instead injecting thoughts into his head; thoughts pertaining to what it knew he'd inevitably find on his journey. While making Johnny believe that those thoughts were his own, it had given him a sort of premonition.

Suddenly becoming aware that he was getting distracted again, Johnny ceased paying the peculiar toilet-fountain hybrid any further attention. Instead, he hurriedly entered the next corridor to his right.

About halfway down this section, Johnny stopped when he saw something unusual in one of the recesses to his left: A narrow, horizontal slit had been cut into the wall at eye level, which brought to mind an aperture used for making discreet observations.

From where he was standing, the opening appeared pretty dark. If he were to take a look through it, he couldn't imagine that anything on the other side would be visible, even if it were worth viewing. At least, that's what his conscious mind said to itself; it was articulating an excuse to reinforce what his guiding sense was already telling him, which was to ignore the aperture and proceed onward.

Just as Johnny was about to step past the recess, he felt a large hand firmly clutch each of his shoulders, pulling him back the instant he'd started to move forward. One of the soldiers moved in front of him while someone restrained him from behind. (Although Johnny couldn't see who was holding him place, he surmised that it was the soldier's identical companion.)

The one in front of Johnny gestured towards the aperture threateningly with a pointed finger, as if commanding him to peer through it. Johnny didn't have time to respond, agreeably or defiantly; the hands had left his shoulders only a second before he could feel arms suddenly wrapped around his torso. Johnny was then lifted up and forcefully brought before the gap in the wall of the recess.

While his body remained tightly restrained, another hand grabbed the hair on the back of his head, and pulled his head upwards. Given a violent shove towards the opening, Johnny didn't have time to close his eyes before the darkness beyond the slit enveloped his world.

# Chapter 9

JOHNNY WASN'T SURE if he was now looking through the aperture, or if he'd just fallen unconscious from having his face slammed into the wall.

Immersed in blackness, the world around him had seemed to dissolve instantly, along with his physical body. While Johnny didn't feel numb, he didn't have any sense of standing on a floor, being restrained, or being pressed into a wall. Actually, he'd lost his sense of having any definite shape at all; it were as though his mind had been torn out of existence and given a metaphysical body of air.

Until now, he'd never had what he could only describe as a conscious blackout… unless this was what he and other people experienced during unconscious blackouts before waking up and forgetting everything about them. Without the ability to recall what happened during an unconscious blackout, he supposed there was no way of knowing what people typically experienced when they were in that state. Maybe the experience varied from person to person, ranging from dreams and visions to a state of non-existence.

After soothing himself with his mental rambling for a few seconds, Johnny began to focus on the feeling of drifting about in nothingness.

He was pretty sure he—or the cloud that his mind was now inhabiting—was moving, though he couldn't tell how fast or in which direction. One moment he seemed to be gently drifting downwards like a freefalling feather, before violently plummeting into an abyss. The next, he could have sworn that he was rising softly like a balloon, before feeling the sudden force of being launched upwards as though he were a rocket.

Every time he was sure he knew where or how fast he was travelling, he would perceive the sensation differently. After a while, he found it difficult to determine the precise moment that his speed or direction actually changed. Either his velocity and bearing would shift the moment he consulted his senses, or the transitions were imaginary.

Then he began to remember things; memories he didn't think he had. Well, according to his guiding sense, they definitely weren't his. However, another presence in his head was insisting otherwise. Unlike the first, that second presence was overbearing and gave him the momentary impression that it existed outside his mind, invading it. Filling his mind with memories that seemed quite real to him, that second presence also insisted that it was just a long-suppressed part of his consciousness, emerging now that the time was right.

His guiding sense, becoming weak and distant, still had enough strength to beg to differ.

Even so, his mind's ear began to hear a low, perpetual drone that had a mechanical and unsettling character to it. The sound was definitely confined to his mind, so he was either vividly imagining it or replaying it in his memory.

Triggering the familiar responses of despair and fear, he honestly wasn't sure if he'd heard the sound before or not. Maybe it was only reminding him of something else; something hazy and unpleasant, which he'd either experienced or imagined long ago.

The domineering presence in his mind insisted that he was hearing a fragment of a suppressed memory, which was now coming back to life. It wasn't just informing him of this; it was filling him with a sense of recognition, eliciting a sensation of déjà vu.

Distant motorized screeches began to echo overtop the ongoing hum. They were almost like the sounds power tools would make if they were being used in a cavernous space, but they had an indescribably organic quality. Come to think of it, the underlying drone had somehow sounded alive as well.

A jumble of brief visions began circulating in his mind's eye, with accompanying sensations; for seconds at a time, Johnny vividly envisioned himself lying on his back, bound to a gurney that was being wheeled through a cold, dark place. Intermittently, he perceived himself strapped to a surgical table, looking up at an enormous room of black metal; flashing screens and bright lights filled his eyes with their harsh glare, making him wince… even though he was pretty sure this was still taking place in his imagination.

Johnny could feel himself being poked and prodded with sharp instruments. A few of those searing stings filled his head with images of unusually large hypodermic needles, which were being plunged mercilessly into his body. Between fiery bursts of pain, he could feel himself growing cold and numb.

Some of the lights actually started to look like eyes. They would always disappear too quickly for him to be certain that they were. However, in those fractions of seconds, he could have sworn that they were attached to what could have been faces. As unclear and dark as they were, he could tell that, at least by human standards, they were grotesque.

In fact, by his standards, they were hideous.

After catching himself making an intuitive distinction between human standards and his own, Johnny felt a surge of uneasiness. Then, as if rushing to answer his oncoming question, something in his mind assured him that Johnny and his kind were familiar with these creatures, long before he'd had personal contact with them.

The intrusive presence in his mind—now acting as his surrogate memory—only referred to them as the Enemy; a race of non-humans whom Johnny had supposedly always feared and avoided.

While he'd been able to look upon these beings once—having done so many times in the past—his surrogate memory insisted that Johnny didn't quite have the emotional stability to do so right now.

Obviously, Johnny wasn't like these creatures, these cruel handlers of his.

Their voices were comprised of the kinds of buzzes, bleeps, and hums that he would have attributed to electronic devices. They were voices, though, and, as foreign as it was to him now, they were speaking a language.

Most of the time they were speaking to one another, though periodically one of them would address Johnny directly, as if lecturing him while he was in a state of semi-hypnosis.

At the time—or so his surrogate memory claimed—he'd understood most of the language, though it had always been a tongue far removed from his own.

Now, he wasn't sure if something invading his mind was giving his comprehension a boost, or if his listening to certain phrases repeatedly had made his limited understanding of the language return. Either way, after reliving certain key reveries a few times—wherein the speech had been slow and clear enough for him to grasp—Johnny was eventually able to translate a little bit of the Enemy's discussion:

"Is the first stage of the experiment complete?" asked one of the voices (at least in essence).

"The physical alterations are proceeding as expected. We are still having difficulty with the specimen's consciousness, however," answered a second.

"In what regard?"

"The creature's mind is resisting our reconditioning process. The more of its contents we replace, the more unstable it becomes. This brain seems to be aware of our tampering and is trying to protect itself; it has become highly susceptible to experiencing wild delusions and possibly other ailments, as if it were trying to alert the creature that something is wrong.

"Do what you can to stabilize the perception the specimen has been assigned."

"What if those of its world discover our activities?" asked a third voice anxiously. "This could be construed as an act of war."

"War was inevitable," answered the first, as if the Enemy had longstanding tensions with whomever Johnny was supposedly associated with.

"It is dubious the creature's counterparts will be able to recognize it, even if they are capable of finding the outpost," added the second. "When we are finished here, it will not even be able to recognize itself.

"Besides, even if its mind does not deteriorate further and it somehow manages to escape, it will still be too engrossed in questioning its own reality to alert anyone of its whereabouts."

Whether or not they cared if Johnny could understand them, they were definitely talking about him. He could have done without being referred to as an "it."

"Once we have finished with it here, it shall be taken to the outpost for study," said the first voice confidently. "Soon, we shall know all that is required concerning the psyche of its kind."

Before the first voice could fully disclose the reason behind the experiment—just what it was these creeps wanted to learn about Johnny's psyche and why—the conversation trickled away into meaningless sounds.

Meanwhile, frozen images and video recordings periodically filled Johnny's head; the sights, and sometimes sounds, drowned out everything he could perceive surrounding the surgical table. In actuality, his mind's eye was recreating the sense of something within the reverie commandeering his mind's eye; mental images were overtaking mental images, almost becoming too much for his senses to handle.

It didn't take long for Johnny to understand that these agents of the so-called Enemy were feeding information directly into his consciousness, while drowning out his knowledge of who he was and where he'd come from. In fact, he began to remember—or at least understand—that the Enemy had actually erased quite a lot of that knowledge.

As far as the Enemy was concerned, Johnny had needed room in his mind to accept a new past, which included a new identity that didn't conflict with his original one, as well as a new world to call home; a world with rich histories and cultures separate from those of his true place of origin.

With that semi-familiar realization in mind, he could begin to deduce the purpose behind the excruciating physical torture:

These beings were changing everything about him, from his anatomy to his very biochemistry, wanting him to reject who he was and accept what they wanted him to be.

Snippets of visions continued to come and go in cycles, giving Johnny an increasingly clear idea of what had supposedly happened just before he'd found himself in a madhouse. Every revelation brought him a sense of recollection that somehow didn't feel genuine; the feeling was an inexplicably artificial form of déjà vu.

Still, he allowed the presentation to run its course, this yarn of his being reinvented inside and out.

From what he gathered, there were two civilizations on the brink of war, each from a different planet. Johnny, whose real name probably wasn't even Johnny, belonged to one of those worlds, while the Enemy belonged to the other.

Neither race was remotely humanoid; in fact, both the concepts of humanity and the planet Earth were fictitious inventions of the Enemy, devised for their experiments.

Johnny wasn't sure what he thought about this whole idea. To the satisfaction of the presence nursing the strange memories, however, he did begin to consider the outlandish premise: After being abducted by aliens, he'd become convinced that he was from a world that didn't really exist, which also happened to be the only home he could remember. He supposed the sudden revelation would have driven him truly and irreparably insane... if he could believe it.

Really, he was convinced that the truth was the opposite of what he was being presented with: This surrogate memory, or whatever it was, was trying to flush his identity as Johnny down the toilet. If it couldn't get him to completely forget all he knew about his life, it would try to make him disbelieve it. As far as he was concerned, the annoying intruder in his head, pretending to help him, was doing what it claimed the Enemy had done; force him to accept that he belonged to a make-believe race of beings from a planet that likewise didn't exist.

As weak as it was, Johnny's guiding sense seemed to agree with that.

The surrogate memory cut into Johnny's thoughts and, without using words, declared that his guiding sense was the result of the Enemy's experiments, which had yet to fade from his consciousness. If Johnny continued to listen to it, he'd not only end up destroying himself, but he would also betray everyone from his world…

Yet, the surrogate memory couldn't remind him of one specific person from his original home. It also wouldn't or couldn't tell him what horrible thing his guiding sense was trying to get him to do.

"So who are you, then?" Johnny heard himself ask in his thoughts.

The surrogate memory stopped giving Johnny further visions, and instead responded with the questionable reassurance that he'd been rescued from the Enemy. Johnny was now in a hospital on his home planet, recovering from his ordeal. According to the surrogate memory, the experience had been so damaging to him, Johnny needed to recover fully before his old life and body were returned to him; his psyche wouldn't have been able to handle the truth all at once. Because of this, those caring for him had given the hospital—and everyone in it—the appearance of the fictitious world that the Enemy had previously implanted in Johnny's mind.

"Wow; that's really going to a lot of trouble for one patient," thought Johnny sardonically.

The surrogate memory went on to contend that the strange phenomena Johnny experienced were due to instabilities in the system that generated and maintained the appearance and workings of everything on the property. Also, Johnny was suffering from minor brain damage, meaning that a few of the unusual things he'd experienced were indeed hallucinations.

Unwittingly, the surrogate memory had just corroborated Johnny's thinking:

He couldn't wholly believe that anything in here was real, and his trusting anything said or revealed to him was a bad, bad idea; that included what the surrogate memory was trying to push on him now.

Needless to say, Johnny was still having trouble with these supposed revelations; either the Enemy's process of re-educating him had been extremely effective, or this whole narrative was the biggest whopper that he'd ever been subjected to.

If it was so dangerous for Johnny to know what he was being shown now, then why hadn't the surrogate memory hesitated to dump all this information on him now? Had this narrative been true, then wouldn't Johnny still be as unfit as ever to learn about what had happened to him?

The intruder in his mind hadn't enlightened him about his past because he was "ready." Johnny had happened into this place by chance after escaping the clutches of Dr. Saunders, whose methods had only made his mind deteriorate further.

Still, the surrogate memory insisted that Johnny wasn't well enough to make a rational judgement of Dr. Saunders. Unsurprisingly, it wanted Johnny to return to his quarters and blindly do whatever Dr. Saunders asked of him.

Faced with two voices in his head, Johnny really needed to discern the truthful one, and fast. If he was truly insane and he couldn't trust any of his knowledge or instincts, then he had no way of knowing what to do… if there was anything he could do. He had to act on the best-founded belief he could muster based on what little he could perceive of his reality.

The cruelty of Dr. Saunders was the biggest hole in the surrogate memory's story, as well as a testament to the true intentions of his overseers. Whoever or whatever they really were, those watching over him had hardly lived up to their claims of wanting to heal his mind, and now body.

The fruits of everything the surrogate memory stood for had already proven rotten countless times; Johnny wasn't going to stomach another taste of them.

For now, his guiding sense was his only aid.

As though his decision had in some way galvanized his spirit, Johnny immediately wrested himself away from the aperture, barely giving it a thought. Instantly regaining his sense of self and place, Johnny looked around and noticed that his two captors (or treacherous bodyguards) were nowhere to be seen.

Although he felt quite shaken, Johnny pressed on, determined to make his way out of the zigzagging passage. For the first time in a while, Johnny was actually pleased; the end of the latest corridor didn't lead to yet another one…

# Chapter 10

INSTEAD OF FINDING HIMSELF in the mouth of another corridor, Johnny was now standing in the entryway of what looked like a large waiting room. The place reminded him of a lounge in a train station or small airport.

The walls, floor, and ceiling were coated in the same coppery alloy that plated the corridors behind him, with spotlights above adding an amber hue to the hazy interior. He couldn't smell anything burning, or see anything in the room that would be giving off the thin wisps of orange smoke that were drifting through the air. In the centre of the room, black padded chairs—most of them occupied—were arranged in four loose rows facing him. Along the walls to either side of him, there were tall potted plants, abundant with healthy green leaves that complimented the orangey-brown hues of the room.

Johnny could see a few neglected arcade and pinball machines here and there, situated in the spaces between the arrangements of greenery. Even from where he was standing—some fifteen paces from the nearest of them—he could see cracks in some of the cobweb-covered screens. In spite of the machines' appearance of long-term disrepair and disuse, the displays were alive with bright, kinetic images. He fought off the urge to take a close look at what appeared to be some harmless video games, which, given his luck so far, would probably bring trouble.

The only people in this large space were nine young men, quietly occupying the seats and giving Johnny the impression that they were a unified group. From the shared look about them, they didn't seem to be waiting for anything. Sitting with a tense upright posture, as if at attention, each had the same emotionless, lifeless expression on his face. Their eyes were open and they were breathing, but Johnny couldn't say they appeared conscious. Dressed in hospital pyjamas that were identical to Johnny's, they were also wearing straightjackets.

Not that he was complaining, but Johnny wondered why he'd never been fitted with one; Dr. Saunders had been willing to do so much worse to him, after all.

A large window stretched across the upper half of the back wall; the yellow glare of sunlight saturated the pane, and yet didn't pour into the room. As he strained to make out any details through the glass, Johnny slowly stepped towards it. For a moment, he thought he could see something against the brilliant yellow; making out a sphere of white light, drifting this way and that, he wasn't sure if he was imagining it. Although his misadventure could have taken him well into the middle of the day, Johnny doubted that he was actually looking outside.

Not wanting to blind himself, he looked away from the harsh brightness, but continued to advance towards the back wall of the room, keeping well away from the dormant patients as he walked around them.

After thinking about whether or not he'd really seen an orb generating all that light, Johnny began to think of the blue light he'd seen spilling through the barred window in the Hole. Unsure of why he made the unconscious comparison, Johnny paused a moment to think about it.

He could feel his guiding sense unlocking a compartment in his mind. It did so almost reluctantly, as if to humour him so he would keep going.

Suddenly, Johnny found himself filled with a rather daunting and unnerving insight; or, perhaps, the willingness to believe a wild tale that he'd just unconsciously invented:

He'd never left the Hole, just as he'd never left the hospital; the two were inseparable aspects of the same place. In one state of consciousness, Johnny would see the hospital as it was, or at least variations of its unstable state; in another, the decrepit and haunted place would become visible.

Without moving from the spot, Johnny was capable of seeing different planes of the same reality, which was indeed very unstable. In order to bring Johnny to the Hole, all Dr. Saunders had to do was induce a particular state of perception; something akin to forcing Johnny to look at a different side of the same object, without actually having to move Johnny or the object.

Johnny realized that he'd been brought to this room in the hospital compound many times, and not once during those previous visits had he been aware that this was the very place he was supposed to reach all along. It really was a shame that it had taken what felt like years for his guiding sense to free itself from his mind, and make that revelation.

Well, he was at his destination now (again), so it was best to get to work... whatever that work entailed.

Shielding his eyes from the light as he came within a few steps of the window, he looked beneath it and saw what he must have been assigned to find:

Just a couple of feet up from the floor, a small keypad was embedded in the wall.

After looking over his shoulder to make sure no one was watching or approaching him, Johnny slowly sat down on the floor, crossing his legs. Closing his eyes, he reached out and let his fingers automatically press the sequence of numbers he couldn't consciously remember.

Johnny was a little startled when, at the end of entering the code, he heard a loud click. To the right of the keypad, a panel, which hadn't been visible until now, slid up to reveal a dark rectangular opening.

He could almost hear his guiding sense forming audible words in his mind:

"You know what you have to do."

Actually, other than reach into the opening with both hands, Johnny didn't really know what he had to do. Yet, the moment his hands were inside, touching what felt like the cables and components of something electronic, he could feel the familiar pull of an old routine driving his hands to act.

Johnny didn't feel the need to peer into the opening in order to begin his task; in fact, his intuition told him that doing so would only distract him from completing his mission. Whatever this contraption was supposed to be, he knew its innards by touch; every piece was where he'd expected it to be before unconsciously reaching for it.

Johnny kept his eyes closed while his fingers disconnected and reconnected wires to and from various ports, flipped switches, and slid what felt like small circuits from one slot to another.

He wondered if he'd practiced doing this on a mock version of this machine; some replica he'd learned to take apart and put back together as quickly as possible. His uncanny ability to perform this complicated activity had most likely come from extensive training, even if he couldn't consciously remember it. Whatever the method he'd used to prepare himself for this, he'd definitely committed the procedure to motor memory; as well as being able to conduct the operation blindfolded, he also found he could do so while thinking about other things, or nothing at all. The experience was a lot like being able to rehearse a song or speech while unconsciously carrying out a morning routine of brushing your teeth, having a shower, and getting dressed.

The idea of having rehearsed this mysterious procedure was comforting to him, since it meant that he was probably doing the right thing. He kept that in mind while he reached into the back of the compartment with his right hand, wrapped his fingers around a small lever, and gently pulled it towards him, which brought his mission to its conclusion.

After pulling his hand out of the opening, Johnny opened his eyes and sighed with relief. Smiling weakly to himself, he took solace in the understanding that he was finally finished… whatever it was that he'd just done.

"Fifteen minutes," he heard himself mutter suddenly; no conscious thought had driven the words out of him.

Had his guiding sense just channelled itself through his larynx?

If it had, it wasn't giving him any indication of what was going to happen in fifteen minutes. However, almost as if it were trying to alarm him, it did bring some pretty disturbing news to his attention:

In this place, a person's perception of time slowed down radically, though also inconsistently. Fifteen minutes in here could feel like fifteen days, months, or perhaps even years. He really hoped that he wasn't supposed to guard the open compartment until those fifteen minutes were up...

While it was stressing him out to consider that he might have to wait here, Johnny did find one thing consoling about this whole time-phenomenon: He probably hadn't been a mental patient for nearly as long as he'd thought... though he'd never kept a precise count of what he'd perceived to be years.

As for the countdown, the only thing Johnny knew about it was that it had something to do with the machine; so, whatever the machine would do in fifteen minutes really depended on what Johnny had done to the machine.

For all he knew, it was about to restart, shut down, or maybe even blow up.

Meanwhile, his guiding sense still couldn't (or wouldn't) tell him anything about the state of the contraption. In fact, that part of his mind had gone completely silent. It didn't seem to care one iota about what he did next; Johnny felt no more compelled to flee the hospital grounds than he felt obligated to wait here and keep an eye on the opening.

He wondered if his guiding sense, a part of own mind, had just betrayed him now that he'd outlived his usefulness.

Johnny remained sitting cross-legged on the floor, frozen from his state of indecisiveness and a little self-pity.

Then a voice—an abhorrently familiar one—suddenly barked at Johnny from behind:

"There you are!"

Before he could turn around to face his old nemesis, Johnny felt the sharp pain of a needle being thrust into his neck.

Without remembering having fallen unconscious, Johnny woke up in a dark room, surprised and disoriented. The first thing he noticed was that he was lying atop what appeared to be a dental patient's chair. His back was raised just enough for him to see down his motionless body, as well as the restraints holding his wrists and ankles firmly in place.

From the neck down, his body felt numb; in fact, he couldn't move it at all, which made the restraints seem kind of pointless.

Though he still could have, he didn't need to turn his head to get his bearings; to his dismay, he knew exactly where he was the moment he saw the barred window on the wall ahead, and the blue glow radiating from the other side of it.

He glanced about the room anyway, confirming that all the disused medical gizmos and junk were still where they always were every previous time he'd regained consciousness in here.

This time, the main difference was that a dental patient's chair had replaced the usual mattress, which filled him with foreboding. Johnny could also see an opening in the wall beneath the window, probably the same one in which his hands had been busying themselves. If it really was the same compartment, no one around here seemed to care about it.

So, he was still on hospital property, and also back in the Hole… or, he supposed, back in the perceptual or dimensional state that made the Hole manifest. Considering the place where he'd last been conscious, he doubted he'd been moved very far in the physical sense.

However long Johnny had been unconscious, it couldn't have been fifteen minutes… at least, not as it would pass in real time. Since time wasn't working properly in here, counting the seconds and minutes was futile, and so was the thought of leaving the grounds.

Perhaps if he behaved himself, he'd be allowed to leave before the remainder of the fifteen minutes elapsed. On the other hand, Dr. Saunders might not ever let him out of this chair, which wasn't good if it was dangerous to be here once that time expired.

A sudden thought came to mind, which made him wonder if he should feel obligated to stay put: If anyone else in here would also be in peril and Johnny had no way of getting the building evacuated, then maybe it was only right for him to remain in proximity to whatever disaster would happen. The idea of escaping while others remained behind didn't sit right with him.

Before Dr. Saunders would be through with him, Johnny was sure he would be praying that the mysterious event would turn out to be a huge explosion, desperate to see his remaining minutes pass as quickly as possible.

Johnny blinked and there was Dr. Saunders, standing to his right. Looking down on him with wide eyes behind his spectacles, Dr. Saunders also had an uncharacteristic smile on his face, which would have made Johnny struggle to break free of the restraints if he'd been capable.

"Don't you remember when the human form was terrifying to you, Johnny? Tell me, when do you remember first accepting your current appearance?" asked Dr. Saunders, sounding as crazy as he looked right now. He didn't seem to care at all about the machine, or what Johnny had done to it.

Johnny didn't answer, too taken aback to say anything.

"Maybe this will help," suggested Dr. Saunders, sounding as though he were convinced he was being helpful. He produced a syringe with a fat-looking needle from out of nowhere, and grinned at Johnny manically. "I'm going to give you a fast-acting antipsychotic."

Before Johnny could protest, Dr. Saunders already had Johnny's head pressed down with one hand and the needle inserted into his neck with the other.

Johnny's felt as though fire were coursing through his veins; he shrieked.

A few seconds later, his body went back to feeling numb, but, when he looked down, he saw that his skin had become green and scaly, while his fingers were now long, wriggling tentacles. He could feel the changes, too; his body grew unnaturally cold and slick, and the bone structure of his face began to feel heavy and out of sorts.

Dr. Saunders threw the empty syringe over his shoulder, and produced another full one.

"To make my point clear, I'm now going to give you a propsychotic."

"You mean a psychotropic... or a hallucinogen... or...?" asked Johnny nervously, his confusion prompting him to ask the question reflexively; he panicked when he realized that his voice was now a coarse hiss.

"If you like," replied Dr. Saunders, giving Johnny a reassuring wink, which, in a twisted sort of way, looked sincere.

In went another needle, and, after suffering another bout of excruciating pain, Johnny looked and felt human again.

"Now, do you understand?"

Johnny didn't even want to try speaking, and he certainly didn't want to indulge the point that Dr. Saunders seemed to be trying to make.

When oh when would the inhabitants of the madhouse tire of insisting that Johnny was an alien, of trying to get Johnny to embrace the idea?

Then Dr. Saunders, after tossing the empty syringe over his shoulder, gave Johnny yet another needle.

"I'm going to give you a fast-acting antipsychotic," said Dr. Saunders, acting as though he were saying it for the first time.

The agony came and went, and then Johnny saw claws growing out of the six fingers and two thumbs on each of his hands; they were also extending from the two large toes he now had on each foot. His skin was also covered in a thick coat of soft white fur.

Once again, Dr. Saunders discarded the syringe and produced another.

"To make my point clear, I'm now going to give you a propsychotic," said Dr. Saunders, again with the same manner and tone as before.

Johnny didn't have time to feel freaked out before he was shrieking in pain again; after suffering through the next few seconds as the drug took effect, his human form returned.

"Now, do you understand?" asked Dr. Saunders.

Johnny responded with something between a groan and a whimper.

Dr. Saunders repeated the cycle of discarding the empty syringe, showing Johnny a new one, and then telling him that it was a fast-acting antipsychotic.

This time, Johnny ended up with a shiny black exoskeleton, four arms, and four legs. He could feel his lower jaw extending, becoming what he imagined were mandibles. Sharp-looking pincers had replaced his hands; they would have been perfect for cutting the restraints if they'd been in reach.

Then Dr. Saunders repeated the other cycle of introducing and administering his "propsychotic," making Johnny appear human again.

"Now, do you understand?"

No, actually he didn't; if Dr. Saunders wanted Johnny to believe that the antipsychotic was revealing his true form, then why was his appearance different every time it took effect? This was just another trick, and a very cruel and agonizing one at that.

Dr. Saunders wasn't giving Johnny any time to provide information, so this wasn't an interrogation…

"I'm going to give you a fast-acting antipsychotic."

"What do you want from me?" demanded Johnny.

Dr. Saunders didn't answer him. The ensuing silence was only broken when the needle drew another scream from Johnny.

Johnny lost track of the creatures he'd turned into over the next while. One was red and gelatinous; another was covered in eyes and thorns. Some resembled sea creatures that had been out of water for too long, while others combined the features of birds, reptiles, and mammals.

For a few seconds, he'd even become a small anthropomorphic griffin.

The pain of the injections hadn't gotten any more bearable over time, and Dr. Saunders hadn't stopped repeating his words and actions with uncanny and disturbing precision. Had it not been for the vividness of the agony, Johnny would have been sure that he was having a fevered nightmare.

Yet, with time, Johnny was eventually able to piece his thoughts together, and remember that this predicament wasn't going to last forever… whatever the point to it was. Between injections, Johnny began to try figuring out the reason behind them:

Did Dr. Saunders want Johnny to submit to the pain and, with glaring evidence to the contrary, falsely accept the idea that he only looked human when he was under the influence of the "propsychotic" drug? Would Dr. Saunders stop torturing Johnny if he renounced the value he placed in a consistent, cohesive reality, and instead accepted whatever absurd notions Dr. Saunders or his colleagues pushed on him? Was Dr. Saunders trying to spite Johnny for whatever he'd done to the machine, even if nothing about it was being mentioned?

Beyond demonstrating how unhinged and sadistic Dr. Saunders really was, the exercise was fruitless. Dr. Saunders didn't seem to want anything from Johnny, who certainly wasn't being taught anything from this. Maybe, as far as Dr. Saunders was concerned, this procedure had no purpose behind it at all; maybe Johnny was incorrect in even thinking that Dr. Saunders wanted him to perceive this as any kind of procedure.

Maybe Dr. Saunders just wanted his patient to be as insane as he obviously was.

Johnny's frantic thoughts and questions began to break down into incoherent mental rambling. Over time, he grew somewhat accustomed to the transformations, and even the pain of the injections. While he hadn't become completely numb to the sensations, he found himself somewhat desensitized to their impact.

Now, he was just staring at the blue light, which was still emanating from behind the barred window. Time ceased to have meaning, and he began to forget what it was like to have been anywhere outside this room. His ability to walk freely seemed like a distant memory, too. Staring at the glow contemplatively, his unfocused thoughts drifted between vaguely remembering that something was supposed to happen, and noticing that the light seemed to be getting brighter, its colour fading.

He was only aware that the blue had gone completely when the now-white light began to fill the entire room, and his eyes.

The routine pains and feeling of confinement stopped, but so had

Johnny's sense of being in any bodily state.

He could almost physically feel something in his mind opening like a floodgate, just before the rush of memories returned to him. Whether it was from the shock of the sudden mental inflow or something else that had just happened around him, Johnny lost consciousness.

However, that fact didn't stop the truth from unfolding in his mind, presenting itself as though it were a narrative in a dream. While Johnny found his tale to be no less bizarre than it was familiar, it still made perfect sense to him...

# Chapter 11

THE STORY ABOUT the peculiar patient in the sanatorium really began with a story about two planets; twin planets, actually.

The orbits of these two planets were the same distance from the Sun, though they remained separate from each other. Their two crisscrossing paths often brought to mind the inaccurate (but catchy) Rutherford model of two electrons orbiting the nucleus of an atom. While the two orbits intersected twice, the planets themselves never collided.

How the planets came to be twins in the first place remained a mystery. Even those who regarded the existence of both worlds as common knowledge still found it a fun topic to think about. No one knew if the two had split apart from what was once a bigger planet, or if each one had been created separately from the same blueprint.

Anyhow, while the pair of planets had been indistinguishable in their youth, they'd yielded increasingly radical differences from each other over the course of their development. Before long, each had its own distinct landmasses, bodies of water, flora, and fauna. Yet, in spite of this, they shared one key similarity that remained unchanged:

Both planets had native human inhabitants. As a matter of fact, there was a massive population of them to be found on each world, possessing its respective plethora of distinct cultures, histories, and technologies.

For the sake of simplicity, people familiar with both worlds called the first planet "Earth One," and its counterpart "Earth Two."

Compared to that of its twin, Earth One had a rather backward human population. While not quite as technologically advanced or—generally speaking—sensible as the inhabitants of Earth Two, the greatest minds of Earth One were still ambitious, and weren't deterred from poking around in things they knew nothing about.

The mighty intellects of Earth One had a reputation for undertaking many high-risk scientific endeavours. Some of which were dangerous enough to threaten even the populations of Earth Two. For that reason, the somewhat-mightier intellects of Earth Two kept a vigilant yet discreet eye on Earth One... to make sure its inhabitants didn't cause too much trouble for anyone (especially those who didn't even live on the planet).

Fortunately for both Earths, and sometimes the entire universe, Earth Two's people were able to watch unseen and, with subtlety, influence the activities taking place on Earth One. Well before Earth One had created its first flying machine, the people of Earth Two had already developed the technology to mask their planet from any satellite, probe, or shuttle that Earth One could ever dispatch.

People from Earth Two could even visit Earth One undetected, which they did frequently.

So, with acute anxiety and high blood-pressure, Earth Two's forces continued monitoring the progress of their demented neighbours on Earth One. On top of conducting surveillance from space, they would also assign undercover security agents to visit Earth One and gather intelligence.

Building secret agencies on Earth One, Earth Two's people blended in with Earth One's population rather easily. All they had to do was infiltrate the right institutions—usually by getting the right jobs—and transmit whatever data they'd collected back to their home world. After learning about a risky experiment or project about to take place, Earth Two's operatives and their superiors would then begin to discus and prepare last-resort contingency plans to shut down whatever might have needed shutting down.

At the same time, Earth Two's people weren't out to stifle their neighbour's innovations or prohibit them by force, which made for a tricky conundrum of what to do when a potential threat presented itself. Practical measures of intercession and prohibition—and the appropriate time of their execution—were actually a hot topic of controversy and ongoing debate on Earth Two.

If their inventions were sabotaged, the people of Earth One would just build whatever they discovered again anyway, while likely learning about Earth Two's existence in the process. Since Earth Two's prevailing voices eschewed both conquest and genocide, they weren't terribly keen on forcing Earth One to do anything that would in turn force Earth Two's hand, thereby escalating a violent dispute.

Besides, as objectionable as some of the planet's citizens found it, Earth Two's policies weren't terribly concerned about what the people of Earth One did to themselves; just everyone else. Some of Earth Two's residents actually relished the idea of Earth One blowing up, whether they outright admitted it or not. Even though most of Earth Two's population didn't share in such radical fantasies, the majority of it was still ready to breathe a sigh of relief the moment Earth One's technological advancement was permanently obstructed. Few would have found fault with Earth One entering a long dark age, wherein technological development either ceased, or, better still, regressed.

With their system of surveillance and covert operations in place, the natives of Earth Two were only marginally reassured. Remaining passively tense, they continued to watch Earth One's progress while doing little about it.

Incidentally, Earth One regularly received other kinds of visitations from the people of Earth Two. This had been going on for centuries, since it was easy for such visitors to get there undetected, and they didn't have to worry about elaborate disguises. Many of the trips amounted to a sort of one-sided cultural exchange program; entire families and other groups would mingle with Earth One's peoples, who in turn would never realize that they and their ways were being studied.

Still, even the visitors and vacationers dreaded the inevitable day when one or more of the civilizations on Earth One would become advanced and reckless enough to do some real damage with their increasingly dangerous inventions and experiments.

Well, Earth One's technologies indeed continued to reach scarier and scarier heights. As time went on, new developments would become increasingly difficult for Earth Two's people to detect. The inevitable day came when one particular series of hazardous experiments began. Those experiments were handled so secretively, Earth Two's forces hadn't known about them until it was almost too late.

Then again, had they known about these endeavours sooner, it was hard to say what Earth Two's people would have done about them, other than continue to watch and sweat with dismay. They had long grown used to refraining from preventing the people of Earth One from making dangerous discoveries. In the same way, Earth Two's people also held back from sabotaging or thwarting the use of anything created on Earth One. It wouldn't be until much, much later that they would finally decide to put their collective foot down and make the firm decision to act; only after realizing that the state of both Earths, and perhaps the known universe, would indeed be threatened by what was to come.

The field of quantum physics had always made Earth Two's people nervous; at least, it did the moment they'd noticed the people of Earth One delving into it. Particle acceleration had played a crucial role in a few of these endeavours, as well as other complicated processes that one could only describe by imparting lengthy and convoluted technobabble.

It would be sufficient to say that, while hiding in deep underground installations, the humans of Earth One had taken to routinely and semi-accidentally ripping temporary holes in the fabric of space and time. Giddy with excitement, they would tear open these voids, which would then seal shut anywhere from minutes to hours later. The consequences of those efforts could have been construed as semi-accidental, because they hadn't really been intended or unintended. The directors of the overall project had just wanted to do what was feasible with the technology they had, and observe what came of their use of it.

Had the observers of Earth Two been watching the experiments, they would have formed at least two opinions about the researchers behind them: The scientists demonstrated little interest in any future practical applications of whatever the work could possibly yield, and their stated desire to learn something conclusive about the universe and its makeup seemed disingenuous.

One day, during one of those increasingly complicated experiments, the Device appeared; a metallic orb made out of an alloy no one could identify. About double the size of a basketball, the surface of the alien object was half-covered in intricate sockets, which appeared compatible with corresponding plugs of human design.

The team who'd found the Device were unsure if it had dropped out of the rift—which should have led nowhere—or if something had happened during the experiment to create the strange object by chance. As illogical as it was, they began to settle on the notion that the Device had just suddenly happened into existence, by accident. Dismissive of the faults in this thinking, they supposed that the Device could have been formed randomly out of the scattered particles of displaced matter around the rift; once the tear in space and time had sealed, the particles congealed into what became the Device. While it was improbable that manipulated matter would simply clump together and reform into something so complex by chance, the small team continued to assert this idea adamantly, refusing to ask further questions about it.

If anyone had been observing them, that observer would have noticed that they didn't really seem to care much about where it came from. Instead, they were fixated on learning its function—as opposed to who made it and why—and what could potentially be done with it.

Every member of that team had been touched by what could only be described as an unholy form of inspiration; an abstract epiphany, which entered their minds simultaneously. While it gave them an uncanny idea of just what they could do with the Device, none of them consciously comprehended the plan they were about to set in motion. Operating like a cult consumed with an obsessive compulsion to build it, plans for a machine were drawn. The Device had not only inspired the design of what was simply referred to as the Machine; it was also to serve as the Machine's core.

With the blessing of their benefactors (and additional funding), the team's work on its original project ceased, abandoned in favour of what became known as "Project Rabbit Hole."

Taking their mystery orb with them, those involved in Project Rabbit Hole moved to a new facility, where no one would suspect any monumental or significant projects to be taking place. A certain state-of-the-art medical complex was a perfect cover for these researchers and engineers to continue their work on the Machine in secret. Since there were plenty of tools and other resources already available on the premises, albeit for medical research, the members of the group also had the space and nearly all the equipment they would ever need.

There, as space was cleared and customized components ordered and brought in, construction of the Machine began. While they remained unaware of what they were making, the members of the team still knew how to make it, which would have only affirmed a popular opinion of Earth Two's people:

For people who were intelligent enough to devise, or even follow, such intricate designs, the people of Earth One really had a penchant for doing inane and stupid things. Once again, the capacity of the best and brightest minds of the planet far exceeded their competence.

The Machine, which had its own generator, had been finished in its entirety within a month of its initial construction. The Device—the Core, as most called it by this time—had disappeared under the complicated network of components housing it, which extended to several rooms (usually hidden behind walls). All that remained was for the mega-contraption to be activated, so the research team would then finally know what it was that this thing did.

Had the would-be observers of Earth Two been privy to this at the time, they would have screamed: "Don't do it!"

Although the Machine was indeed activated, no one behind Project Rabbit Hole got the chance to learn anything about what it actually did.

Even if those curious minds had been capable of figuring out what had happened, they still wouldn't have had the time to solve that mystery before finding themselves engulfed by something beyond their comprehension.

Less than a minute after the strange instrument had been turned on, a wobbly translucent and luminescent dome encased the medical complex, which then began to emanate strange sounds and pulses of light.

Needless to say, the nearby locals of the surrounding city became rather concerned about the appearance of this anomaly—more so after the disappearance of the initial responders, who'd been last seen entering the property to investigate.

Meanwhile, phone calls made to any department in any building of the complex would be answered with eerily calm replies. Wondering what all the fuss was about, receptionists on the other end of the line continually asserted that everything on the grounds was fine and operating normally.

Because of the appearance of the dome and the disappearance of emergency responders who'd approached it, an alert was eventually issued. High-ranking authorities were notified, and a secret task force was assembled and assigned to secure the area, as well as deal with what was no doubt a threat.

"Project Rabbit Hole" soon became "Operation Rabbit Hole."

The task force overseeing the operation was comprised of top specialists in the military and scientific fields, assigned by the highest of Earth One's human authorities (among them the original benefactors of Project Rabbit Hole). Although its members were the most qualified to identify and take care of the phenomenon—or so thought those in charge—no one in the task force actually knew anything about the problem.

The luminescent phenomenon, and the area around it, had been sealed off in a state of quarantine. The only ones allowed near it were members from that special unit. Those who got close enough to its perimeter to investigate, however, would disappear, just as the first responders had.

Still, phone calls to anyone inside the anomaly would always be answered. Between politely offering information or a referral to another department, the receptionist would always sound baffled at the mention of a state of emergency.

Meanwhile, Earth Two's observers had an idea that something disastrous was taking place; at least, after their attention had been drawn to the sudden happenings at the medical complex. Not wasting any time, they immediately set to work on figuring out the nature of the phenomenon. Their advanced equipment allowed for quite a thorough investigation, which could be conducted from a safe distance. Fortunately, most of their methods could be carried out from space; some even as far away as the surface of Earth Two.

One of the first things they realized about the anomaly was that it was regularly emitting strange colourful pulses of energy. Every couple of hours, a cluster of them would emerge from the dome, flying upward like sparks. Then, they would soar across the planet in every direction, behaving like comets, before falling to the ground. Upon impact, a circular wave of energy would stretch outward from each point of collision for a few miles before dissipating. To anyone watching them from above, the waves resembled the rings that would form in a pond after someone dropped a pebble into it.

The rings affected the stability of any matter they came in contact with, transforming entire areas—and everything in it—into something completely different. In other words, some strange property of those rings was able to destabilize and then reconfigure matter, altering living and non-living things into radically different and improbable beings and objects. People and animals would become organisms that were stranger than mythical beasts, while entire towns would turn into ruins of civilizations that had never existed anywhere in the known universe.

Then, minutes later, everything in the environment would simply return to its original state.

The type of change in a given environment seemed to be random, though other factors could have influenced it… Perhaps a sentient mind within the anomaly was conveying the blueprints of its imaginings through the pulses, whether doing so consciously or unconsciously. It was also possible that the conscious or unconscious thoughts of those in an affected area could have played a role in the nature of the transformation.

The transformations were fleeting, and nothing living or non-living had been permanently changed, or left damaged by the fluctuations. However, as time passed, those changes began to last longer and affect greater areas, and had the increased risk of becoming permanent. The affected matter also needed time to lose its plasticity, and it was hard to say how many times the same area could be affected before permanent damage was done to it.

The bursts from the anomaly were also gradually becoming more frequent. Earth Two's investigators didn't know for sure, but they strongly suspected that the anomaly was sending them out deliberately, whether their respective destinations were purposefully selected or random.

Earth Two's investigators also reached the well-founded hypothesis that similar instabilities were probably occurring within the anomaly, even if the receptionists inside were somehow kept unaware of what was happening to them and their environment.

Those investigators also noticed that the border of the anomaly was growing. Although its perimeter was only expanding about one inch a day, they knew that there was no reason to be complacent. Without anything done to stop the process, those daily inches would inevitably add up to the area of the entire planet.

Before the anomaly got a chance to consume the planet, its routine shower of pulses was going to remake Earth One into something unrecognizable or a giant ball of self-moulding putty. Doubting that Earth One could withstand such ongoing instability, the investigators believed that—if Earth One did become a giant hunk of clay in a state of perpetual metamorphosis—the planet would eventually collapse and disintegrate.

Earth Two's people might have dismissed the problem, deciding that

Earth One was getting its just desserts, but there were two problems with that:

The first problem was that the whole of Earth One could eventually turn into something autonomous, and dangerous for the rest of the cosmos… perhaps a giant space monster with nuclear missiles for teeth, which would then flash a big smile in the general direction of Earth Two.

Then there was the second problem…

It didn't take long for the minds of Earth Two to realize that something was happening to their own planet, as a direct result of what was happening to Earth One.

Now, there is this popular and silly notion that human twins share such a deep bond that when one of them experiences something, the other can somehow empathetically feel the same thing from afar. If one is in danger, the other feels afraid, and so on…

Sure, such a notion might be either amusing or irritating in the eyes of human twins (and rightfully so). Unfortunately, however, the twin planets of Earth One and Earth Two weren't in a position to scoff at the concept so easily.

While there was no visible anomaly on Earth Two, or even pulses of energy, the transformations were still occurring all over the planet's surface, at the same times and in the same relative locations that they were on Earth One.

Something else was happening to Earth Two:

An unseen force was trying to move the planet from its orbit, as if tugging it in the direction of Earth One. Each pull, which resulted in small worldwide tremors, was subtle; but, with the means they had, Earth Two's scientists were certain of what was happening. While the disgruntled investigators couldn't say for sure if the anomaly had something to do with it, they were pretty darn suspicious that it did.

While Earth Two was being dislodged from orbit, the effects of the anomaly—or perhaps the anomaly itself—seemed to be protecting the planet from any cataclysmic changes to its atmosphere and terrain. In any case, the world was somehow being preserved, albeit in preparation for a collision with its twin. The absence of an immediate worldwide disaster was only a minor consolation in light of the planet's slow and unnatural shift out of orbit, not to mention the existing crisis that both Earths now shared. No one was going to be grateful to the anomaly for protecting the world's inhabitants from the effects of a problem it had ultimately caused.

The scientists and leaders of Earth Two weren't sure what would happen by the time the two planets collided, since both planets would likely be in a state of complete plasticity once they were in proximity to each other. (None of those scientists or leaders wanted to visualize the two inhabited planets as malleable balls of mud, which were about to be squished together, but they couldn't help themselves.)

Hoping that the anomaly could be given a concrete and precise identification, a separate team of researchers on Earth Two searched for any record of an occurrence that was remotely akin to the threat that both worlds now faced. The best they could unearth were old entries about similar, rare phenomena appearing in the planet's ancient history, though none of them had managed to affect the entirety of one planet, let alone two. The accounts were fragmented in that they didn't—or perhaps couldn't—identify what any of those phenomena actually were, or where they came from. Until facing this new phenomenon, most people had regarded the old tales as myths or embellished legends.

With a collective shrug, the researchers supposed that what they had managed to find was still better than nothing.

Interestingly enough, the rather vague history made a point of dismissing the idea that anyone on Earth Two had brought those anomalies to their own world, whether deliberately or accidentally. So, while a few of Earth Two's ancient peoples had supposedly encountered phenomena like the current one, those encounters had occurred purely by chance.

From the wording of the sketchy accounts, it seemed as though the ancient historians of Earth Two had been looking into the future, eager to push a narrative for their descendants to adopt: No one on the planet would ever do anything to wittingly or unwittingly invite such a problem, let alone worsen it with dangerous cult-like practices. Implicitly, that narrative insisted that no one on Earth Two had ever been as daft as Earth One's dimwits had constantly proven themselves to be. Even in ancient times, a significant amount of people on Earth Two seemed to be fond of saying things like, "Earth One's most brilliant mind is still a dim bulb."

The anomaly in every story had been described as a living, sentient creature. If the similarities between the current phenomenon and those of the past held true, then the people of the present were dealing with a problem that was not only alive and dangerous, but also something that could be solved... though with extreme difficulty, and only with the cooperation of Earth One's task force.

Saving the remaining mythological scraps for future briefings, the research team compiled their findings with those of the other investigators, and prepared to pay Earth One a visit.

Before approaching those in charge of Operation Rabbit Hole, however, Earth Two's investigators had also made a point of acquiring detailed confidential information about Earth One's recently-assembled task force. Specifically, they'd collected plenty of information about its capabilities and its members, which most people on Earth One were barred from knowing anything about.

A good week after the medical complex had been put under quarantine, Earth Two's emissaries finally decided to brave introducing themselves to the task force. These delegates then made Earth One's clandestine crew a conditional offer of assistance, which some might have called an ultimatum:

If the task force would keep its mouth shut about the mysterious extra-terrestrial humans and their resources, then the extra-terrestrial humans would offer Earth One their support, and keep their mouths shut about the task force.

Needless to say, the leaders of Earth One's task force did not want the existence of their group to be known to the vast majority of people on their planet. So, after listening uneasily, they could only reluctantly comply.

Earth Two's representatives went on to issue a warning, which some might have called a threat:

Earth Two's people weren't to be trifled with, so anyone on Earth One with nefarious ideas could forget about capturing, studying, dissecting, or vivisecting any of their representatives.

So, a deal was made and (some) information was shared.

Earth Two's people were willing to tell Earth One's that the anomaly was a living entity and it was connected to the Machine. The Machine could have pulled the creature from another dimension, or could have served to sustain the abstract life form, perhaps after having created it. It was also possible that the Core of the Machine had served as its home or prison. It didn't matter, since, in any case, the Machine was still its lifeline, whether it was literally giving the beast life support or only keeping it linked to the corporeal realm on Earth One.

Hopefully, if the Machine were to be shut down, the anomaly would go away, and its effects would wear off before any permanent and undesirable changes to Earth One occurred. (Earth Two's representatives didn't bother to mention what was happening to their own world.) They honestly couldn't say if shutting down the Machine would erase all of the problems, but it was the only thing that could be done.

Finally, the visitors from Earth Two told the task force that, before taking part in Operation Rabbit Hole, they would need to examine the blueprints of the Machine.

After the task force reluctantly agreed to hand over a copy of the plans, Earth Two's agents studied it carefully and realized just how complicated the design of the Machine really was. The thing had been built to be monumentally difficult to shut down; they would need to spend time training someone to deactivate the Machine under psychologically gruelling conditions.

Earth Two's representatives did not want to waste any time, especially since the training process would already create a worrying delay. So, they recruited someone who'd already received the specialized mental training required for withstanding intense psychological attacks, with

which the anomaly would no doubt bombard an unwanted infiltrator.
That was when they'd decided to summon the Agent…

# Chapter 12

WHEN HE WAS a boy, the Agent had moved to Earth One with his parents and siblings. There, he'd grown up while he and his family had moved from city to city. He'd spent most of his years in North America, though, for whatever reason, his parents had also insisted on making stops in and out of other nations within the Western Hemisphere.

The Agent hadn't cared for the Earth One name he'd been given, which suited the English-speaking regions in which he'd spent most of his time. All the same, he'd become more responsive to his alias than he had to his true name, which filled him with resentment; he didn't like the idea of a counterfeit identity overshadowing his real one, especially since he'd already hated living on Earth One.

All throughout his travels on the planet, the Agent had encountered more problematic people than he could count; they'd shaped his rather bleak perception of the world and its native inhabitants.

Whether he was at school, dealing with various professionals, or, later on, interacting with employers and co-workers, he'd experienced a variety of issues, which, for all their differences, were strikingly similar. It would have been an understatement to say that he'd met people who hadn't said what they'd meant, or hadn't meant what they'd said. Many of them would actually revise what they'd said or meant, thereby changing the claims they'd made initially.

After imparting a new interpretation of their meaning on a selective basis, they would claim that it was the only interpretation they'd ever wanted him to make. Though he knew better, they would suggest that he hadn't understood them properly when he'd heard them speak their words the first few times.

Eventually, the Agent had come to feel as though the world around him (or perhaps the particular individuals he'd had his closest interactions with) were trying to stifle his ability to see them and their intentions clearly.

Maybe he'd just been unlucky when encountering people, always at the wrong place and time. Maybe those whom he had such unpleasant dealings with hadn't represented the majority of the population.

Then again, perhaps those areas of Earth One had been filled with a mentally and spiritually poisonous social climate, brimming with sordid ideals; an indulgent prevailing culture that celebrated meaninglessness, self-contradictions, and flightiness. Whether or not the prevalent norms and ideals were a part of the culture in any formal sense, they certainly weren't compatible with the values he'd been brought up with.

Providing people with a means to deceive one another and discard responsibility in favour of decadence, the cultural current did seem to lean towards abolishing the concept of absolutes for one to trust in.

To him, it had often seemed as though the social architects—and those who embraced their ways—just wanted to kill any sure footing his perception of the world around him could have. As it was, he would always doubt any seemingly concrete understanding of what people meant whenever they did or said something… especially when it would prove inconsistent with whatever they would say or do moments later.

As the problem worsened, his qualms about the reliability of his senses intensified, and so did his wariness towards those with whom he interacted. Eventually, he'd stopped fretting and had instead come to anticipate inconsistency—or his perception of it—from people before they would actually demonstrate it. He would watch and listen carefully during every interaction he had with someone, making sure he perceived everything that the person said and done correctly. He would then await an oncoming irregularity or revision of intent, preparing for the moment when he would have to decide if he was going crazy, or being deceived.

Whether consciously devised that way or not, the prevailing culture flooding the areas he'd visited had seemed at least permissive of that distasteful side of the human condition. Maybe the area's social norms had been consciously tailored to exacerbate the problem, even by removing commonly-understood meanings behind (and precise definitions for) concepts, actions, and anything else that expressed a significant idea or intention to another person.

The Agent really didn't like the way that the value of meaning—as in, a definition of a concept and the weight it possessed—appeared to have been arbitrarily replaced with a draw towards ambivalence. He didn't care for the loss of consistent definitions for concepts like "truth," "love," "loyalty," "compassion," "right and wrong," or even "meaning." Not only did he witness such concepts stretched into meaninglessness, after being selectively redefined so many times, but also their trivialization, the loss of their value.

The apparent complacency many people had with this was also bothersome. It seemed to him that some of those people just didn't want commonly-understood, clear definitions for their words. A few of them also appeared to want the value of certain concepts diminished, albeit arbitrarily. He noticed how they still wouldn't hesitate to reverse their position on this, however; though they did so whenever it suited them. He would catch people covertly redefining words like "fairness" in mid-conversation to help hide the reversal, while dishonestly pretending that no such revision had ever taken place…

After dismissing or objecting to the idea of treating someone fairly, those individuals would then hotly object to the reality of receiving such treatment themselves. When their double standard was pointed out to them, they would try to revise the terms of the conversation with an absurd redefinition of "fairness." They would perhaps insist that the word—to them—meant blindly distributing all credit or treatment equally; in other words, universally dispensing rewards and punishments, no matter what the recipients had or hadn't done to earn them.

As much as they would deny it, they knew that their application of that word was disingenuous, and had never been relevant to the conversation. They knew that both sides of the debate had initially been using "fairness" as a synonym for justice or doing right, which entailed due credit for work and effort, or specific accountability for wrongdoing.

He would also catch people suddenly exaggerating the difference between pairs of concepts, like "fairness" and "justice": If he made the supposed mistake of using the word "fairness" instead of "justice," then his true meaning—and whatever problem he cited—would be dismissed.

Seething, the Agent could see why people like that would love to stretch the meanings of such words further and further, until they could mean just about anything (and ultimately mean nothing).

On top of this, the Agent really had trouble with the emerging demand for meaningless things to be taken seriously, as though they should have been treated as meaningful, no matter what. To him, this was a lot like saying:

"I'm proud to be a born liar, and I renounce the concept of truth. However, unless you're cynical and nasty, you're still under the obligation to believe everything I say… and treat it as though it were true!"

He'd seen that thinking infect every aspect of society, from the arts to personal relationships. With pompous pretences of sophistication, deluded elitists vocally celebrated the creation and display of useless and tacky objects in the art world… apparently because they were useless and tacky. (Instead of challenging a problematic status quo honestly, it seemed that these people preferred to see the complete rejection of substance—and the concept of objective reality—spread throughout the whole of civilization, even if gradually.) Meanwhile, after trivializing or even discarding the significance of human relationships, plenty of people became self-important and pretentious about their frivolity and debauchery (which entailed the use of those whom they devalued).

On one hand, such an insidious cultural movement could serve as a cheap excuse for people to embrace their narcissistic tendencies, which would otherwise be regarded as manipulative, dishonest, and hypocritical.

However, he often doubted that most of these people would consciously give their behaviour that much thought. At best, they'd cite some ideology to excuse themselves, after doing what they probably would have done anyway.

As far as the Agent was concerned, the appetites of what he regarded as decadent bloodsuckers had made the unsavoury cultural movements and norms popular, and not the other way around. Even so, he'd found it increasingly difficult to believe anything his senses told him. No matter how explicit or self-explanatory a statement—or even a friendly smile—would seem, he would force himself to abandon his natural interpretation of it. If his perception had actually been wrong as many times as he'd been led to believe, then perhaps he couldn't rely on his perception to discern the true meaning—let alone authenticity—of anything happening in the world around him.

Now, because longwinded sob stories would detract from the point of this narrative (and because the Agent himself dislikes thinking about these things), any further details are best left undisclosed.

The important part is that, before he was twenty years old, he'd had a nervous breakdown from prolonged social maladjustment. The Agent had been suffering from what could only be described as a perceptual crisis, which was not to be confused with an existential one. He'd completely lost faith in his ability to interpret what he saw or heard with accuracy, no matter how substantial it might have seemed to his senses. During that period of his life, the Agent had come to doubt his ability to perceive the ground on which he was standing, or even the fact that he was really standing at all.

He had tried visiting the mental health professionals on Earth One several times, but the experiences had only helped marginally. While he was able to get through his schooling, and survive one transitional odd job after another, the torment always came back. By the time he'd reached twenty-two years of age, the Agent had returned to Earth Two a disgruntled, misanthropic, and paranoid wreck.

To his amazement, the therapy on Earth Two had proven much

more effective. (It didn't hurt that the prevailing culture on that world was more to his liking.) During that time, the Agent had learned about specialized techniques that the people of Earth Two had developed to enhance their psychological stability.

He'd also learned about advanced techniques of controlling one's own mind, using methods that Earth One's people had never even dreamed about. (Even if Earth One's people had dreamed about such methods, they still wouldn't have been able to realize them; the internal biology of Earth Two's humans did have slight but significant differences, which included aspects of the brain.) Training in this art of mental self-discipline had been usually reserved for soldiers and other fields requiring extreme self-discipline.

That was what had inspired the Agent to enlist and eventually become, well… the Agent.

With newfound determination, the Agent had begun his training as a soldier in his homeland—his real homeland—on Earth Two. To his surprise, the structure and exercises of boot camp were strikingly similar to those of Earth One's forces (at least, from what he'd seen and heard). Aspects of his stay at the base were so familiar—in an archetypal sense—that he could have easily imagined himself back on Earth One doing the same thing. (To his irritation, his personal mental images of archetypes, especially those relating to people and their occupations, had long since been drawn from Earth One's versions of them.)

He'd marvelled at his being able handle what he'd initially thought would be unendurable conditions. Then again, there'd been context there to justify whatever he'd gone through, no matter how gruelling. For a start, he knew his superior officers were yelling at him because he and the other recruits needed to get used to unforgiving conditions. This was significantly different from the time when he'd awkwardly watched an unprofessional supervisor's curse-laden temper tantrum in the backroom of a grocery store; the outburst had only come because the manager in question was having a bad day.

Anyway, the Agent had worked his way up the ranks and eventually joined a special operations branch, where he'd finally received the degree of mental training—and peace of mind—he'd sought.

Whether it was a reward or punishment for gaining mastery of his emotional problems, the Agent had been chosen for the mission of infiltrating the anomaly and shutting down the Machine.

Incidentally, the given name of the Agent was Gryphon. Though it rhymed with "hyphen" when pronounced correctly, Gryphon knew that his name—when written in one of Earth One's alphabets—could bring to mind one of the planet's mythical beasts.

# Chapter 13

THE VOICE IN JOHNNY'S imageless dream finished its story just in time for his state of unconsciousness to give way to semiconsciousness. A reverie of overlapping and vivid memories filled his mind, both replacing and completing the narrative.

Did he actually believe all the freshly-materialized junk that was now in his head?

Yes... yes, he did. Wow; he really must have been off the deep end today...

In spite of the condescending and almost sardonic tone of the narrator (who'd sounded suspiciously like Dr. Saunders), Johnny accepted the tale he'd just heard in his sleep.

If nothing else, he now had the complete memories to support the account.

He wasn't sure where he was lying down presently, or if and when his body was planning to awaken fully. Deciding not to worry about such things for the moment, Johnny didn't bother to try moving. Remaining on his back, he instead relaxed and allowed his thoughts to drift about in his head.

Snippets of his briefing and the mission kept coming back to him:

Johnny and his superiors had suspected that the anomaly would at least put up the front of an operational medical complex within its boundaries, sanatorium and all. For that reason, he'd prepared himself to assume the role of a newly-admitted patient, matching the creature's pretence.

If Earth Two's fragmented lore held true in the case of this particular creature, then it could probe the minds of anyone who entered its perimeter. So, Johnny had needed to shield his mind with the techniques he'd learned to save himself from becoming a real mental patient. The moment he'd entered the grounds, he'd seen that everything appeared to be the way it was normally. At that point, he'd immediately hid the truth of who he was from both the creature's awareness and his own.

The fact that he'd actually suffered from acute anxiety had made believing in his new identity rather easy; the heavy bag of emotional garbage he'd carried for the better part of his life (thus far) had made his role a natural fit.

Just before his self-programming had become active, mere seconds after he'd entered the premises, Johnny had been a little concerned about whether or not his mind would properly unlock the right information at the right times. Sequences of specific thought processes were to act as the combinations; he'd trained himself to have the right emotionally-charged fits of introspection long before he'd first engaged in them. Once that training had been done, he'd then had to lose his awareness of the plan; he couldn't afford to retain any conscious memory that related to his intentions, the real reasons behind his stressful contemplations.

Johnny remembered feeling quite apprehensive over whether or not those sequences would still come to him at the right time, since he would perceive the thought processes to be natural. (They were quite similar to what he'd experienced for real, back in the days when he'd actually been suffering from anxiety.) In fact, he'd fretted endlessly over the many ways the plan could go wrong… until the moment came when his memory had finally been blindfolded.

It was funny in a way; Johnny never would have thought he'd see a day when he'd actually wanted to suffer his recurring thoughts about his hang-ups. Yet, he was bound to have those ruminations whenever he spent too much time alone, making them the mental processes of choice. Sure enough, they had indeed served as the perfect key.

During a long and in-depth briefing, Johnny had been told something else that he'd found interesting, though a bit unsettling: Even though hospital receptionists could still communicate with the outside world in real-time, there was a good chance that Johnny would think he'd experienced more time in the anomaly than he really would. (According to the ancient accounts, that occurrence had been the case with the other anomalies.) He wouldn't age faster than anyone outside the anomaly, his superiors had said; and, neither he nor anything around him would seem to act with dramatic speed or sluggishness. His superiors couldn't explain the temporal issue, or how it worked, but they'd done their best to present him with a loose, hypothetical comparison:

"Picture all activity in an enclosed area suddenly experiencing the same boost of acceleration, while everyone in that area is also experiencing a perceptual slowdown, each to the same degree. So, to those people, everything in their hastened world appears to be moving at a normal speed... When they step out of that area, they are surprised to learn that their experiences of the past few years had actually taken place within the span of an hour."

Straining to see the positive side of this idea, Johnny had considered that he would have more time to complete his mission than he would ever need. For that reason, Johnny had tried not to worry too much about how quickly he could reach the correct combination that would, among other things, awaken his guiding sense.

Presently, Johnny wondered how long he'd actually been in the sanatorium; at least, in the eyes of those who were outside the anomaly.

Piecing together what he'd been told during the briefing and what he'd experienced during the mission, Johnny also realized that there'd been two types of beings residing within the anomaly:

The first were the ordinary people who'd either been on the premises when the anomaly consumed it, or had entered it after the fact, most likely to investigate the strange occurrence. Putting it lazily, they would have ended up under the anomaly's spell, either in a catatonic state of waking dreams, or playing whatever role the creature assigned to them at whatever given moment; possibly roles that the creature had devised for them. Perhaps the contents of a victim's mind played a part in defining his or her precise role; or, perhaps the creature drew ideas of how to reinvent a person from what it gathered from the minds of others.

No matter what, everyone would mindlessly readjust to any change of circumstances, believing the new histories they were given; staff would accept new patients, who were probably old patients with new respective appearances, health issues, or identities.

Meanwhile, the visitors who weren't hallucinations—whether they'd originally been visitors, patients, or staff—would probably be drowning in the delusions the anomaly was pushing on them. With their sense of time and place constantly being meddled with, they would likely be restricted to thinking that they were leaving the medical complex or had just arrived. Continuously walking in and out of buildings, to and from parking lots, they would be unable to realize that they'd never left the grounds, and were incapable of leaving.

Based on what Johnny had actually ended up seeing—now that his mission was over—he doubted that most of the people in the medical complex had changed outwardly completely... Sure, some of the doctors might have become patients, while visitors might have become security guards or nurses, but it was plausible to think that everyone who was originally human had likely kept a human appearance. However, he couldn't say one way or the other if anyone had ended up with any significant physiological changes, such as a new face, a radically different age, or something else just as drastic.

Surely, no one had become inhuman... Johnny certainly hoped that no one had, anyway. He doubted that the odd animal or autonomous machine he'd come across had once been a person. It sickened him to imagine that any coffee cup or piece of paper, which he'd crumpled up and discarded, could have once experienced personhood.

Comparing his experiences on the grounds to the plans and pictures of the place—which he'd studied before going in—he could safely say now that the anomaly had kept most of its immediate environment the way it had found it. For that reason, he was a little reassured of what he still wanted to believe about the people in the affected area. (He couldn't begin to guess why the entity had exercised any self-restraint when it came to the complex, since it hadn't been so conservative when it had been influencing the rest of Earth One, and the whole of Earth Two.)

Then there were the other beings that inhabited the anomaly, which were neither human nor illusions. The lore of Earth Two suggested that these smaller entities had always been a part of the main creature, inseparable yet distinct from it. In hindsight, many of these sub-creatures had probably been hiding in plain sight, mingling with the captive humans while disguised as patients, visitors, or staff. Even if and when they hadn't taken human form, they would have been impossible to distinguish from anything animate or inanimate within the anomaly, he supposed.

With that thought in mind, Johnny had to reconsider his notion—his hope, really—that no one human had become inhuman while under the macro-entity's influence. As much as he'd tried to dismiss the unpleasant possibility, he had to consider that the real humans could have been manipulated to appear as alien as the sub-creatures actually were.

The apparitions, mutants, and other oddities could have easily been humans, sub-entities, or illusions. The same could have been said of that pink moose, though Johnny considered that it might have been an animal of some kind originally, like a lab rat or squirrel. (If that were true, maybe some of the people or apparitions he'd encountered had once been animals as well.)

If anything could have been made to look and act the way the macro-creature consciously chose—or randomly selected—then any affected human (or animal) in its grip could have been made into an expressive extension of the entity. It was depressing for him to imagine the degree of control that this anomaly was said to have over minds, which supposedly had free will. If the beast really could reduce unwilling parties to mere puppets so easily, then Johnny wondered what separated the anomaly's captives—humans or otherwise—from its possibly-mindless residents, the sub-creatures.

The anxieties saturating Johnny's current thoughts reminded him of the worries he'd experienced as a child, after he'd first heard about topics relating to hypnosis and mind control. To him, those kinds of invasive influences were even eerier than a megalomaniac's deceitful attempts at indoctrination or social engineering, which said megalomaniac might have tried to pass off as mere enculturation.

Without knowing much about such spooky subjects at the time, Johnny's imagination had run wild with upsetting thoughts about them. He'd become preoccupied with the disturbing idea that a person could be programmed like a machine; his or her consciousness made to act, feel, desire, or become just about anything the manipulator wished.

Even in his early years, he'd asked himself questions in a state of panic: If an outside force—person, machine, or something else—could easily transform your mind into whatever it desired, what did that say about who you really were? Specifically, what did that say about the authenticity of your character? If that outside force were to transform an identity utterly, did that mean the death of the original identity… or did that mean the original identity never had a solid existence? Johnny had wondered how stable or real a person's character was… especially if anyone could come along and rewrite it as though it were computer software.

Before actually learning more about such topics, Johnny had fervently longed for confirmation that his first impressions were either grossly inaccurate or false. He'd desperately wanted to know that an outside force couldn't simply erase a person's will or radically change it, and had clung to the idea that perhaps some people were impervious to such forms of programming. As for those who weren't completely immune to forms of mind control, he'd hoped that there were still limits to how successful nefarious attempts to reprogram them could be. He had really wanted to believe that such attempts couldn't make people feel or desire things they didn't already; or, make those people do things they weren't always willing to do.

In those days, he'd dreaded the concept of getting close to those who could be programmed to hate the people they loved, or betray those to whom they'd professed loyalty, or do anything that went against their convictions. Had he not been so miserable, he might have laughed at himself for having wondered if there were ways to test people around him, in order to see if he could trust in the stability of their nature.

(The mental training he'd later undergone was not the same as what he'd once feared. It was merely a tool, which had always been under the control of his own will. For that reason, it had nothing to do with fundamentally changing his character.)

He didn't remember when or how exactly his fears had been alleviated, or what consoling information had since come to his attention, but something had eventually brought him out of that state of misery. However, the anxiety he'd felt back then was returning to him now.

Johnny resumed thinking about the recent past, and he suddenly remembered what his superiors had said to him before he'd entered the anomaly, which intensified his unhappy state: The only key difference between the human puppets and the sub-creatures was that the sub-creatures were irrevocably bound to the main anomaly, possibly birthed by it. Johnny's superiors had proceeded to tell him that, unfortunately, there would be no detectable difference between influenced humans (who could have been disguised as something else) and sub-creatures (which could have been pretending to be human, or something else).

Perhaps, he hoped, those briefing him had been wrong… Maybe there had been other differences between captives and native inhabitants of the macro-creature, even if Johnny hadn't been able to spot them. He would have liked to think that it wasn't so easy for the anomaly to remake certain things completely, such as the people who weren't already a part of the abstract beast. Unlike controlling the sub-entities, maybe transmuting and manipulating a human being was a difficult and complicated process for the creature. Perhaps the success and degree of transforming someone depended on a variety of unknown factors, such as the state of the subject whom the anomaly wanted to transform. Maybe, just maybe, it wasn't always possible for the anomaly to transform a person that much, in body or mind.

Theories about the sub-creatures were brimming with conjecture, but had still been interesting to him, though in a gloomy sort of way:

One theory suggested that the sub-creatures were once-separate beings, which had since been abducted, partially absorbed, and then permanently bonded to the creature. If that were true, then the human puppets would have probably become similar sub-entities if they had remained in the anomaly long enough.

Another theory purported that the sub-creatures were akin to small organisms that lived within or on bigger organisms, whether they were symbiotic or parasitic in nature. In that case, their presence in the macro-creature was similar to the existence of bacteria naturally found in the human body, the barnacles on a whale, or maybe even the fleas on a dog.

According to the lore, the sub-creatures worked cooperatively with the main creature, and could have been the avenue through which the anomaly drew information from conscious minds. In that case, the sub-creatures were likely empathic or telepathic to some degree, possibly serving as middlemen between the macro-entity and any captives it enveloped. Whether the sub-creatures were directed by or cooperatively controlling the main anomaly was anyone's guess; perhaps each side took turns.

Perhaps the main creature and its sub-creatures were all parts of a kind of gestalt; a single entity made up of seemingly separate yet undeniably connected parts. Perhaps the sub-creatures were little more than a set of appendages and sensory organs for the anomaly. In that case, perhaps they only manifested as autonomous beings whenever the macro-creature prompted them to do so, whether out of necessity or desire.

Before beginning the mission, Johnny had been especially mindful of the existence of the sub-creatures, and what they could do: He hadn't needed any lore to understand that, of all the beings he would interact with, the sub-creatures would be the ones to scrutinize his consciousness the most. (He'd also imagined that this would certainly be the case if they acted completely on behalf of the macro-creature.)

He'd realized that anything he knew, felt, imagined, or had locked away in his cognition could be pried out, interpreted by them or the bigger creature, and then used to influence a radical shift in the entity's domain. The more personal his interaction with one of the sub-creatures (whether verbally or in his thoughts), the more easily they could draw from his psyche.

Remaining in his semi-reflective reverie, Johnny now began to contemplate the entity's consciousness, and the idea of whether or not it could really be called a consciousness in the conventional sense…

Like the anomaly itself, none of its natural inhabitants (or appendages) necessarily had a personality or underlying character of its own. If each of them based its apparent, sometimes-fleeting identity entirely on whatever the strongest psyches in proximity offered, then he wondered what distinct characteristics defined its decision-making process; or, what defined its choice to draw from one particular facet of a subject's psyche over another.

Without boasting, Johnny could say that his mind had probably been especially attractive and inspirational to the anomaly and its components, since his psyche was abnormally resistant to becoming enslaved by the entity.

Johnny fought off the idea—and ensuing panic—that perhaps he only believed he'd resisted the creature's influence. A part of him was compelled to wonder if the entity wanted him to believe that he'd been capable of resisting it, which meant that he was doing its bidding now…

For all he knew, Johnny's slight differences from the other captive humans might have naturally drawn the anomaly and its minions to him, and maybe that was why the creatures had refrained from invading and transforming his mind and body directly (for the most part). Perhaps something in his psyche had given the creatures the particular indication that he was unusual; his latent self-consciousness of being in some way "alien" to Earth One's people.

In their own alien way, the macro-creature and its smaller counterparts might have only been trying to learn more about Johnny.

Their attempts to antagonize him could have been a form of studying him, he supposed; through their antagonism, they certainly had drawn a lot of information from his head.

On the other hand, the entity and its underlings might have wanted to test anyone on the premises, since all humans would have been aliens to them. Maybe Johnny only differed from the rest because, deep down, he believed he did; the anomaly might have reflected that thinking without having any firsthand awareness or understanding of it.

Maybe their exploration of psyches in general had come out of curiosity or malicious intent. In the latter case, they could have wanted to draw things from minds that would direct the course of that maliciousness, especially if they weren't particularly inventive or creative themselves. Perhaps these creatures naturally assumed the role of a tormentor so they could somehow feed on whatever anxiety or anguish they managed to draw from a target… Perhaps the entity and its minions believed that torturing alien specimens was a great way to learn the most about them.

Johnny also considered that maybe the creature and sub-creatures' exploration of psyches was akin to an instinctive animal impulse. In that case, the otherworldly elements haunting the medical complex might have only been mimicking what a part of Johnny's mind had expected them to do. A part of him had assumed that they were out to dig around in his mind for information or to antagonize him, so maybe they'd only responded to his thinking without awareness, assuming the role which Johnny's psyche had fed them.

Whether or not the anomaly and its smaller representatives had simply emulated having certain conscious intentions towards him, they might have had another purpose behind their actions thus far. They could have been keeping that purpose a secret; or, they had an aim that was so otherworldly, no one from Earth One or Earth Two could begin to fathom it.

As it was now, the intentions of the entity and its inhabitants were definitely beyond Johnny's comprehension, which emphasized just how alien—in every sense of the word—the creatures really were. The question of the creature and sub-creatures' conscious or unconscious purposes yielded innumerable possible answers; too many for Johnny to think about further.

The point was, well before arriving here disguised as a patient, he'd known that these things could likely become tormentors, whether intentionally so or not. He'd found it overwhelming to think about... The entity and its servants could draw anything from his or any victim's mind, ranging from unpleasant memories to subjectively defined archetypes that were likewise displeasing to that victim. These strange beings—or their host—would then compound the contents of Johnny's psyche, and bring them to life as physical (or ghostly) costumes for the entity and its servants to wear. (In hindsight, Johnny was surprised he hadn't had a worse time in the anomaly than he'd actually had.)

Before beginning his mission, Johnny had also kept in mind the possibility that not everything in the anomaly would be out to harm or deceive him. He hadn't found it difficult to consider that some of the sub-creatures could easily manifest as the non-threatening contents of his mind; or, bring to life a composite of combined memories and ideas that weren't particularly bothersome, doing so only because they were in his head to be realized. In that case, the entity would be mirroring aspects of who and what a subject of scrutiny was, bringing to life surreal abstractions that weren't anything more than a confusing externalization of the subject's—his—mind.

In fact, if these entities really were instinctively exploring minds without knowing what they were doing, he'd considered that they might have unwittingly become useful things from time to time. With a little bit of optimism, he'd imagined seeing manifestations of pleasant memories, helpful people, or anything that reflected his positive frames of mind (such as they were).

From what he'd learned over the course of the briefing (which had since been proven well-founded), Johnny had known that—no matter what infuriating thing he could experience inside the anomaly—any negative emotion could bring disaster on him. Before beginning the mission, he'd set out to prevent any feelings of violent anger before they could start.

His solution had seemed so ingenious at the time, which had involved the use of his special training. Normally the mental process was used to keep himself calm in stressful situations, but, with a little adjustment, he'd really pushed it to the next level… Like redirecting a current, he'd been able to shift his intense feelings away from angry emotional states (those which could make him become physically violent), and towards the emotional states of a hyperactive or obnoxious child.

His reasoning for that approach had been pretty straightforward: What could be more innocent than a child? What better state of mind was there for him to adopt if he wanted to vent any excess energy, without receiving horrible feedback from the anomaly?

Sure, he'd kept in mind that any goofing off or hyperactivity could have yielded other kinds of unpleasant feedback, and that his entering such a state could distract him from what he was supposed to be doing. However, it was the only way to hold back whatever internal darkness the anomaly might have found in him to exploit, which would have definitely made the situation worse.

Now that the worst was over (hopefully), he was in a position to look back and say that he stood by his initial reasoning. Although he'd slipped up a little, and went through some gruelling experiences as a consequence, his regressive fits had ultimately saved him from experiences that he wouldn't have been able to cope with.

Completely purifying his mind of all inappropriate or angry thoughts would have been impossible, no matter what. As it was, he'd been so rushed during his other preparations for the mission, he hadn't had time to master the art of unconsciously turning his childlike regressions on and off at will.

(Among other things, he'd also had to keep disassembling and reassembling a replica of the Machine, which his people had thrown together for him to practice on.)

193

He'd known that there was a chance that the regressions could be triggered sporadically, sometimes when he wasn't violently angry. He'd also considered the possibility that the process would wane or begin to falter over time.

Looking back, he felt blessed that the process had worked as well as it had.

Johnny, unaware of where he was presently, suddenly realized the potentially fatal error he'd just made:

The more aware this place was of what he'd so painstakingly tried to conceal, the more its defences—or reflexes—would act up in harmful ways. Thinking about what his mind had concealed from him would have put him in danger...

If he was still in the heart of the anomaly, he was putting himself in danger right now.

Oh dear...

Johnny's heart and stomach sank for a second, before something occurred to him:

Wasn't it supposed to be over now?

Wondering if the plan had actually worked, Johnny's anxiousness sent a vigorous rush through his body, making it just lively enough for him to open his eyes. Though he was still extremely tired and feeling as though something heavy were weighing him down, he was at least properly awake now.

He was lying on a bed, in what looked like the private room of an ordinary hospital.

A pair of armed soldiers guarded the exit off to his right.

A few paces away from the foot of the bed, a group of familiar-looking men stood, talking to one another excitedly as they took turns glancing at him. If his memory was accurate, some of them were his people and the rest were Earth One's people...

The man he remembered as the leader of the Earth One task force was the first to notice Johnny staring at the group of them.

"Agent Saunders," he began, giving Johnny a formal but enthusiastic smile, "You're awake. We have good news…"

As the self-important man and the others took turns debriefing him, Johnny half-listened while trying to be civil, holding himself back from looking terribly disgusted with these Earth One folk. He didn't try too hard, though: Between the gross irresponsibility of the planet's leading scientists and Johnny's generally lousy experiences with the general population here, he wasn't in the mood to hide his contempt to the point of straining himself. Besides, he was so groggy that any involuntary scowls of his would probably be interpreted as signs of extreme fatigue, anyway.

In spite of his contempt, he was relieved to hear them say that the mission had been a success. What was codenamed the Rabbit Hole—the anomaly—was gone. The task force's head science guy cheerily told Johnny that it was a little early to say for sure if the effects of its presence would dissipate completely, but his team was confident that there was nothing to worry about.

Of course, his people would have to run tests, and see what they could discover at the site of the medical complex…

The man and his colleagues looked a little too confident and complacent for Johnny's liking. Those who'd summoned the entity had probably carried themselves in a similar way, which expressed the kind of single-mindedness that gave rise to carelessness.

Had he the energy to do so, he might have said, "Yeah, how quickly you eggheads forget recent events, like when you'd lost your composure the moment you realized you weren't the lords of nature. You guys went from cocky to looking ready to soil yourselves, and now it looks like you're going to revert to cocky mode again." The scornful words in his head were as clear as anything he could have spoken aloud, too.

Then again, nothing he could say would likely make any meaningful impact. If anything, he probably would have sounded like a preachy schoolteacher to their ears.

Tuning out the babble in the room for a moment, Johnny began contemplating his current circumstances. He didn't know how to be sure that he was really out of the anomaly, and that brought a rather upsetting possibility to mind: What if his current situation, or his understanding of it, was just another trick of whatever nasty presence or presences were infecting the sanatorium? Actually, he didn't even know if those excruciatingly slow fifteen minutes had truly passed.

The immeasurable span of time he'd spent in that dental patient's chair had felt like an eternity, and thinking of it made his skin grow cold. Immediately, he forced himself to bury the memory, which was both distant and recent.

A small part of him was having a little trouble accepting what otherwise felt like his real life. For now, however, Johnny would settle on what seemed apparent to him; presently, he was just too tired to worry about answering deeply unsettling questions.

Unfortunately, once he had the energy to examine the unnerving possibilities thoroughly, he was sure he'd be having anxiety attacks for a long, long time.

The head of Earth One's task force suddenly broke Johnny's train of thought with a statement that was particularly hard to ignore:

"We hope you and your colleagues have had a pleasant-enough experience on our world," he said, looking a little awkward and frightened under his pretence of diplomacy. His words had actually sounded more like a subtle plea for mercy than they did a gesture of sycophancy.

As for the time Johnny had spent on Earth One, well…

There was a lot to be said about the life he'd lived here, but he didn't want to think about that right now.

# Acknowledgements

A big thanks to my anonymous support base (including my proofreader) for their assistance in my times of need.

You know who you are.

I would also like to thank Arwen K. from Lulu.com for thoroughly answering my many, many questions, thus making this crash course in self-publishing a little less daunting.

# About the Author

**Tall Pike** is the codename—or, if you like, penname—of some guy who decided that his purpose in life was to create stuff. Although the "stuff" in question mostly consists of prose and music, he does approach (stumble through) the world of visual art on occasion. In fact, his piece, *Gryphon's Identity Crisis*, adorns the cover of this book… and the door of his parents' refrigerator. He is also responsible for the mostly-electronic music project, **Perpetual Sensory Overload**, which, to date, spans four albums (available digitally… hint, hint). Tall Pike lives somewhere in Canada, and was indeed born on planet Earth… or so it is commonly believed. *A Mad World in a Madhouse* is the first of his books to see the light of day, though—be warned—there are more sitting on his hard drive, which he plans to unleash on the world in due course…